A SAFE PLACE

STEPHANIE CARTY

Print ISBN: 978-1-917449-36-6

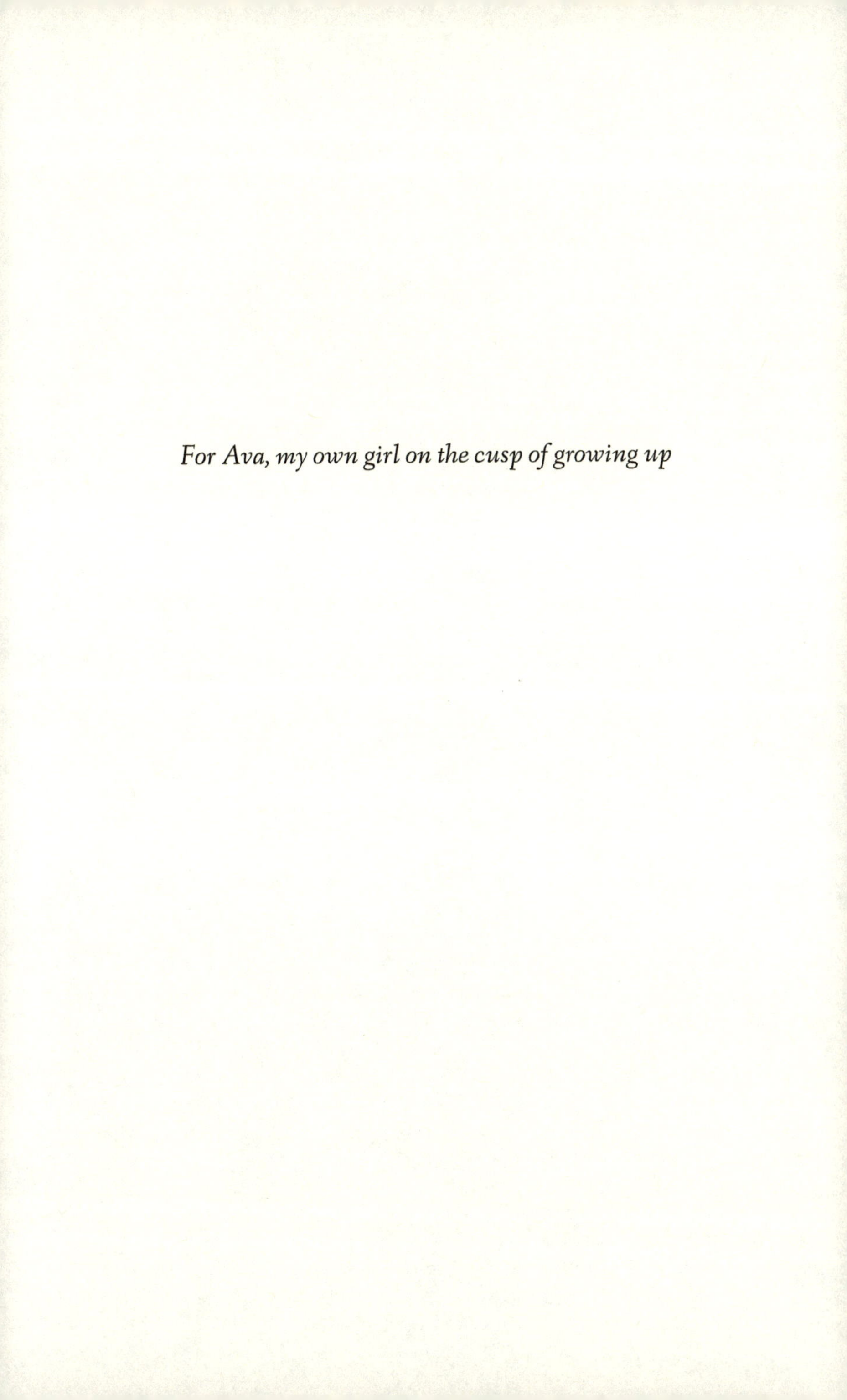

For Ava, my own girl on the cusp of growing up

1
———

CATE

The sun is almost at its highest point in the sky which means it's the middle of the day. I like middles; not too much and not too little. I like to be middling. I'm a grateful girl, that's very important. I have Mam and our village of Halham – the two best things. That means I don't need anybody or anywhere else. I pinch the skin on the back of my hand to try to stop the next thought from coming again but it comes anyhow. Not exactly a thought with words in sentences that can be put in order. More like a tunnel. If I look through the long, long tunnel in my mind, I spy things that I haven't seen in real life yet. I spy with my little eye something beginning with O.

Outside the village.

I can't quite imagine what it looks like because I don't know what there is past the woods and farmland. There must be other villages of course, and far bigger places like cities that are still in England. There's Rome and Greece, although they're not ancient anymore. There is Notre-Dame cathedral, the Pyramids, chocolate factories, soldier barracks, graveyards, the desert and ginormous boats that float on the surface of the sea because of physics. There are babies and girls the same age as me and fathers and millions of people who might be sitting in their villages right now, wondering what other places look like or sound like or smell like, and whether it's true as Mam says that there's no place like home.

My thoughts are far too whizzy. They push hard against the side of my brain making my head thump. I need to slow everything back down to focus on one thing. I turn on the garden tap and let the water trickle over my hands, turning them frontways and then back. The water is cool and clear. I let my thoughts come out of the pores on my palms then wash away.

The thoughts flow down the drain into pipes that take them into the centre of the Earth. There, the letters and sounds will disintegrate and become fresh soil full of ideas, ready to nourish our fruit and vegetables. That's why it's good to talk to things that grow. But not now. I need some quiet time. I switch the tap off and watch the drips for a little while longer. Drip, drop, drip.

The month is probably May. I figured it out by sneaking a look at the sowing instructions on the packets of runner beans while Mam fetched a trowel. She told me once that Mayday is a special word that ships and aeroplanes use if they're in trouble – *Mayday, Mayday!* It sounds fun rather than dangerous but words can play tricks like that. It reminds me to check for any aeroplanes coming through the stripey clouds. Sometimes they fly low over the village to keep an eye on us down below.

The runner bean seeds are big. I hold one up to the sky to see what's inside but it doesn't give away any secrets of how it grows and changes so much. I push each one about three finger-widths into the soil at the bottom of a cane.

If time went faster – I *wish* time would move faster – you'd see them curl and climb right up the cane. The beans will be long, green pods that can snap in half to show the babies tucked up inside.

My finger bones click as I press a seed down. Mam is out in

the village so instead of ignoring the pain to not worry her, I pull my finger. *Oof*, that feels better. Until the next time.

My hands are floppy and tired out but I need to write my questions down so I don't forget them. Mam says I ask her too many questions so I should list them in a notebook to see if I can figure out the answers myself. But now I know a secret; I know what the farmer's phone can do.

Mam called out to Farmer Grove across the field to ask when the cows would be going back out to pasture. They spend winter indoors, bored and cold, even though they have each other. We love to watch them when they return outdoors in the spring, as playful as pups, running and nudging their heads together before chewing fresh grass. I saw Farmer Grove take his phone from his pocket saying he'd check. I know phones can make calls to people in other places but this was different. His fingers darted over the screen. Then he shouted that it would be Wednesday as that would be a dry day. The phone knew!

Since then, my brain has been extra busy so that more than once Mam has asked, 'Are you in the land of the living?' and I thought, well, that is a good question for my list.

One day, when Mam's out of sight, I'll ask Farmer Grove if I can borrow his phone. I'm not allowed near him or the farm helpers without her there but she's so busy in Halham that I'll find a chance. I must be ready with my questions.

How many Mays have I been alive for?

How many Mays does Mam have left before she's very old?

How many Mays did Grandfather have before he died?

How come Mam had a father but I don't?

I wiggle my sore fingers and move my pen to rest on a different part of my thumb.

When I'm grown up, will I be able to safely leave the village?

How will I know when I'm grown up?

Mam doesn't like measurements. She doesn't mind fuzzy

ones like fingers and cups and afternoons. But she doesn't like precise divisions like years or miles or October the tenths. She'd say, 'Time doesn't like being chopped up that way' and frown a little, her voice low and fast as if it could overhear us.

Mam's right that time doesn't always pass in the same way. It moves strangely. Sometimes it leaps ahead like rabbits darting over the fields; sometimes it's as slow as a runner bean winding its way up a pole. The problem is that I can't answer any of my own questions about time because in Halham, time is as floppy as Mam's tape measure. The numbers have rubbed away so she pens little marks on it to make pieces of fabric the same length for our clothes.

I don't know how old I am, so I can't do the maths of how long until I'm a grown-up – which Mam let slip is eighteen years. That's her worst number. I don't think she has a best. Maybe it's two, like mine.

My long plaits feel heavy at the side of my head. The green gardening scissors that rest in my hand would make it so easy to snip-snip them both off, but Mam would be upset. She said it would break her heart into pieces if I cut my hair, that it's mine to treasure. It doesn't feel like a treasure. It feels like stinky straw that pulls on my scalp and makes my neck ache.

But I don't want to do anything to ever make her upset again, not like with the baby bird. We are best friends forever which is called BFF. I draw a quick heart with BFF in the centre of a page then slip my notebook back into the pocket of my dungarees and clean up the garden tools, ready to see how pleased Mam is with me when she comes home and I show her all I've done.

2

IMOGEN

NOW

Imogen hadn't intended to walk so far from her home and daughter but once she was halfway up the hill it seemed important to finish what she started. Out of breath now at the summit, she rests one palm on the rugged trunk of a tree. Their house of glass and metal looks out of place down below, nestled amongst old stone and wooden structures. It had seemed the right choice at the time – a new building to banish the ghosts of her history.

The ache in Imogen's legs is a welcome distraction, but she hasn't shaken off her unease. Tomorrow is her daughter's thirteenth birthday and even though Cate doesn't know it – can't know it – it's as if she senses that she's on the cusp of change. Cate's body is beginning to stretch and alter from the small, soft child that Imogen could provide the perfect life for: a woman-in-waiting. It's all gone far too fast. The ideal moment to pause time has already passed.

Instead of recovering her breath now she's still, Imogen finds herself gasping, as though she has climbed a mountain not a hill. The air thins to insufficient for her sea-level lungs. She shouldn't have pushed herself to walk so far. Her health has never fully recovered from those childhood years of doing the Rounds with Father almost every day. The damage is done. She'll suffer for this in the morning. Her knees give way so that she crouches on her haunches. The house is no longer in sight.

Elastic between her and Cate seems stretched almost to breaking point at this distance. They are rarely apart; home holds them together. Imogen forces herself back up to standing. She traces the outline of their house. It's too big for just the two of them but there will never be anyone else there. She'd designed it that way to ensure they had room to breathe.

To the east is the vegetable patch where Cate will be concentrating on her planting tasks this morning, her lips pressed together tightly in determination. Cate has a slender frame but she has strength in different ways.

When Cate was born, Imogen was reborn, so it will be both their birthdays in a way – the mark of years of survival. No, more than that. She should celebrate the anniversary of their special bond and contentment. Other things, too; darker, necessary things. But there's not much that can be done about that.

Imogen stamps the mud from her shabby boots. The soles may not make it through another winter but they'll do for now. There's no reason why she and Cate can't continue to have a good life together. She needs to make some adjustments, that's all – some allowances for Cate's age which she hadn't really thought through all those years ago when she made the biggest decision of her life. Imogen knows she must find a way to change some of the rules while maintaining a line that mustn't be crossed.

From high above the house and farm, Imogen feels more lost as to how to deal with her growing girl. For some reason, she wishes she could ask Father for advice. It makes no sense at all given that his choices prevented Imogen and Cate from living a normal existence. Yet, she craves to hear his voice after all these years. It had a calm certainty to it back when she was the same age as Cate is now. As if travelling back in time, she can recall in detail the back and forth between them when she was on the cusp of womanhood herself.

Father had laid his heavy hand of concern on Imogen's back while she was fully immersed under her blankets, avoiding what the day was meant to bring.

'I know you're tired but today's important.'

Imogen clutched on to the ends of the covers in case he tried to unwrap her. 'You *always* say it's important, every time. I want to stay home today.' The itchy material scratched her skin but that was at least her own choice. 'You said we could start digging out space for the vegetable patch.' Imogen tried to keep her voice calm and steady but she could feel her throat closing up in protest, which squeezed her words into a whine.

Father sighed and Imogen felt the weight of his disappointment start to crush her ribcage.

It had been different when she was a toddler. Doing the Rounds with him seemed fun, all part of a game in which she was the most important person in the room – the one they all clamoured for, teary-eyed with wonder. It was different now she wasn't a little girl. She didn't want to traipse from place to place; crumbling cottages and cold village halls awaited. Homesickness drenched her with each excursion. It was getting harder to leave the house for each set of the Rounds. She no longer craved outsiders' admiration. Imogen yearned to snuggle into the nest of home. To read, grow food in their neglected garden and worry about nobody but herself.

'I promise we will make time in the garden tomorrow. We could get some clippings while we're out. You can choose any flowers you like.'

Once again, she felt unheard. Father confused his wishes

with hers. Imogen didn't care for flowers as he did. As soon as they arrived, the inevitability of their wilting caused her to avoid looking at them. She wanted to grow her own bright tomatoes and strawberries – to nurture nourishment and rely on nobody else at all. Her dream was for her and Father to stay home together with uninterrupted lessons and time in the garden with the gates bolted shut to the world. She tried to imagine what it would be like if her energies and choices were her own, rather than belonging to lonely outsiders who stole her precious time.

'I don't want to. I'm tired. Everything hurts. Doing it makes me hurt more.'

How many times had they rotated around the same conversation recently, as if playing a game of catch? In reality, they never played games; there was no time for unnecessary frivolity, only *important work* to be done.

'Immy, you know that a little ache or tiredness is a small price to pay for the good you do for others. You can rest in the car. It's only a couple of hours away this time. They'll be waiting.'

He never showed anger. Imogen had tried – God knows in months of hormones and frustration – she had tried to provoke a different response. If only he had shouted and bullied. If he forced her into action rather than pressed on her guilt, she'd have had something to rail against. But the goodness in her father was boundless. Imogen poked her head out from the blanket and savoured her father's smile. Her resolve slipped through her fingers.

Father held up his hands. 'Okay, okay, I know, you need your space to get ready! See you downstairs in fifteen minutes?' His smile was soft under his moustache.

Imogen wanted to keep this playfulness between them but the thought of the years ahead was suffocating. 'I can't keep doing this until I'm eighteen. It's too much. I want to do other things, be normal.' She knew what his reply would be as if they were both reading from scripts that couldn't be edited.

'Being special is better than being normal. Better for everyone.'

Under the blanket, Imogen rotated her sore ankle. Yet another sprain while her work took its toll on her body.

'It's not better for me.' Her voice came out as tiny as her hope that it would make any difference. Imogen couldn't look at Father when she spoke out against his plans. Although she had every right, it always felt as if she were sticking a knitting needle in the chest of the person she loved most in the whole world.

'I know it's not an easy path. I'm so proud of you.'

At the top of Hart Hill, the wind changes direction, bringing Imogen back into the present. Her hair blows about wildly. She gathers it together around her fist and refuses to think about a time it didn't belong to her.

3
______

CATE

I've been learning about different types of scientists. Each has its own special name that ends with -ologist. I think Mam tries to be a Cateologist, the way she watches what I do and how I react, even though she tries to cover it up by sewing or humming at the same time. She studies me.

One science lesson, I read something about the tiniest particles in the universe. It's one of those lines that I said over and over in my head until it stuck.

The act of observing influences the phenomenon being observed.

I asked Mam if I was a phenomenon and she laughed, curling her hair behind her ear and said I most certainly was. So, when Mam observes me, I must be the very best girl I can be. Then she will carry on loving me most of all and her sadness will stay away.

Sometimes we sit in the study to do our lessons but on sunny days we do learning outdoors.

'Which areas of science that we discussed would you like to focus on?'

I take a moment to make it look as though I'm thinking of

the answer because Mam says it's not healthy that I do so many lists in my head. She says children don't need lists or order, that they should play freely. But I guess I have my own ways of playing. I stare at one thing which is how to look thoughtful. The goldfinches dance around the bird-feed holder that I made in the woodshed last year.

'I think maybe it's archaeologist, palaeontologist and zoologist.'

Mam raises her eyebrows which means she's rumbled something. 'Interesting how they came out in alphabetical order.' She smooths her apron down a couple of times but she doesn't frown, so it's all okay. 'What activity are you going to do today that relates to one of those?'

My toes wiggle. That means time out in the village while Mam is busy with chores. I try to keep my excitement still so her detective eyebrows don't rise again. She's trusting me more to come up with my own learning tasks away from the house. I mustn't ruin my chances by not being careful with my words.

'If I do a bit of digging, it could be all three! I might find an old coin, or fossil or a new type of worm.' I meant to mix the word order so the examples weren't following the alphabetical list but my brain doesn't like that because it makes me feel icky. I speak quickly so Mam doesn't have time to notice. 'I'll take the bucket and magnifying glass then go in the corner of the field where the old bench is.'

This is on the far side, away from where the farmers may walk this afternoon while they tend to the sheep. Mam understands and nods, her hands already busy with the next task of sorting her seedlings.

'I'll look forward to hearing about your discoveries.'

That's the way it works with us. We tell each other things in code. She worries about me, so I let her know I'm following the rules. I worry about her, so she lets me know she's not upset.

That's a good way to do it when you're not allowed to touch each other. We hug with our words.

With the whole afternoon free, I take the long route around the village. The road into Halham starts in the west which is where the sun goes down. Mam has a car parked next to the house but she doesn't go in it often because we have everything we need here. I follow along with my head facing forwards in case Mam is watching but my eyes flicker right to see if anything new or exciting is there.

Once I found a kite tangled in the brambles that must have flown here from far away. The fabric was ripped and there was no note sewn into it but it was a thrill to touch its surface and wonder who had played with it.

There was also the time with the baby bird here but I don't want to think about that so I focus on the crunch of gravel under my feet.

The corner shop is past the old stone walls where all kinds of bugs crawl. I'd like to pop in but Mam hasn't said we need anything from there today so I scoot past and run my fingers along tree branches that lean over the whole length of the wall.

The holiday house is tucked behind shrubs and a cluster of trees so that only a corner of it shows. Mam says it's 'chocolate box'. I know it isn't made of chocolate but sometimes I pretend it's the house from *Hansel and Gretel* with walls you can eat and a scary witch who locks you in, ready to make you into broth. It would be good if I had a brother – we could push the witch into the pot and save each other, then eat the tasty walls.

Mam says to only make up happy stories but they come into my head however they want and besides, we're in the safest place in England. There won't be anybody staying in the holiday house yet. They only come in the summer. My heart does a little extra badabam-badabam when I think about it. There are no other children in the village. This summer will be my chance to get a friend, I'm certain of it, now I'm given more freedom to be out by myself. Perhaps I'm nearly a grown-up? The top of my head reaches Mam's nose now.

The far end of the village has the best view. Hart Hill slopes up from woodland to the skyline. Bushy trees like broccoli make it green all over. Hart means a male deer. There are red deer peering right now that I can't see but I feel them. I know they're watching over me with their antlers ready to fight off anything or anyone bad.

The buildings in this part of the village are older than our house. The row of cottages, the outhouse, the farmer's barn. In the evenings, Mam goes down there with farm goods for the neighbours who are too old to get their own food and milk.

In the centre of the village is the playground I've loved since I was little. There's a metal swing, a tyre swing, a see-saw and a climbing frame. The best is the tyre swing because you can park your bottom in the hole so it holds you tight, then close your eyes, leaning back slightly. Mam used to push the tyre but now I can make it swing myself. I don't mind going high. It doesn't scare me.

I never go on the climbing frame. It used to make Mam tense up and say it was time to go home, telling me to watch my left foot or hold on tight. Atoms of her worry travelled in the air so that I'd swallow them down, making me feel sick if I even tried to climb the bottom rung. Instead, it makes a good castle or igloo. I can climb between the bars and nestle inside. If I could lay eggs, I'd use it as my nest and wait while they hatched.

The oldest couple in the village are on the edge of the playground now, nudged close to each other, dressed in their best clothes. Some days I chat to them but today I'm so eager to start my science trip that I wave and keep moving.

To the east is the farmland, green as far as I can see. The nearest patch is ours then further out belongs to Farmer Grove's family. Mam likes him. She says he's a quiet man which means he's not into our business. He has different types of cows but my favourites are a reddish colour. I'm not so keen on the noisy sheep, apart from when they have their baby lambs.

I find a sheltered spot behind the wall to lay out my spade, sticks, notebook and magnifying glass. I guessed right that the magnifying glass was passed down through the family because it looks old instead of shiny like most of our stuff. Its handle is silver with swirls and flowers. Mam said it belonged to Grandfather's mother, who was called Margaret.

I haven't asked any more questions yet because it's better to save them up and sprinkle one or two a week, otherwise Mam gets stressed and starts to pick the skin on her fingers and tell me to be quiet. I do know that Margaret lived a long time ago because Grandfather was quite old to have a baby, whatever that means. I've divided time into *now, recent, old, antique* and *ancient*. I think that my great-grandmother and the magnifying glass are *antique*.

I lie down on my belly and slip my shoes off so the tops of my toes are tickled by the grass. Or maybe it's my toes that tickle the grass? I like to get right down on the soil to see what it would be like to be as tiny as an insect.

The blades of grass wiggle to and fro in the breeze as they chat to one another. I lay my head to the ground to listen to their whispers. Eavesdropping is against the rules but I think that's only for humans. I learnt about how bees communicate by dancing but I'm pretty sure that grass does, too. A combination of the gentle sound and the way they bend towards each other most likely. Each blade talks to the next, and the next one after that. The messages can travel a long way really fast, especially when the wind picks up. I listen hard and watch the nearest blades. One day I'll learn their language and send my own message back across a hundred fields, ready to be heard by somebody else's ear pressed down on the ground far away.

Daisies decorate the meadow here. I looked up *daisy* in our old English-French dictionary because it's the only one we have. The pages are yellow and the red binding has pulled away from the spine. Its copyright says 1903 which I think is older than Grandfather. The dictionary says that daisy is "marguerite" in French which sounds like my great-grandmother's name.

This is one of the most important things that I have noticed: everything is linked one way or another; you just need to wait until you find the strands between them. Mam showed me how to thread daisy stems together to make a necklace. I tell the daisies a story that is about them.

The daisies wonder why me and Mam can't touch each other. Although I notice they don't either, spread out along the grass too far to reach one another. It's a tricky question. I should probably add it to my list. I don't have the answer but I do have a way to explain it. Saying one thing is like another is called a metaphor. It doesn't tell you *why* but it does tell you what it feels like, which is almost as important. I try to explain to the curious daisies. It may help them, too.

I used to have a wooden train set that we laid out across the study so I could play while Mam did her accounts or read a book. If you tried to stick the red engine to the wrong end of a carriage, the magnets would push each other away, even if you really wanted them to go together. That's called repulsion. However close I want to be to Mam, or her to me, instead there is repulsion: a push away no matter what we do. There's no point being sad about it because that won't change our magnets. Instead, it's better that we spend lots of time near each other without trying to touch, and I keep busy in my head with learning and lists and stories.

The daisies nod that they understand. The grass between them dances.

I find a patch of earth where the greenery is sparse, ready for excavation. An archaeologist looks for artifacts, which are things that humans made. They get left behind when terrible things happen or everyone moves away. A palaeontologist looks for very old creatures like the fossil Mam found on Hart Hill of an ancient animal, spiralled in stone forever. To find the old things you have to scrape away one layer at a time. If you dig too deep you may miss something or accidentally break it apart.

I'm not even one finger width in when I hear the farmer's helpers. They're about half a field away so can't see me. Unlike Farmer Grove, they like to chat and laugh. Sometimes the tall one with brown hair punches the shorter, blond one on the arm, but not in a bad way. They laugh and tumble about like the farm dog's puppies. I try to focus back on my patch of earth. I angle the magnifying glass to check for tiny fragments. Although I try to concentrate on my work, it's as though I've got an extra eye on the top of my head still watching the men.

Mam wouldn't like that. She'd say 'Men are different to us. They can smile while they lie. They're dangerous to girls because they only see the way the world is for men. We don't need them.'

I want to ask whether Grandfather was dangerous. When Mam mentions him, I can't read her face like I usually can, the signals are scrambled.

The farmer's helpers have finished their work on the tractor and step out into the sun. The dark-haired man has taken his top off and tied it around his waist. He has a striped torso as if his muscles have been drawn on all the way down to the top of his jeans. The men are laughing as they get nearer to where I'm sitting. I don't move. I can't move. I stay low in the grass. I'm glad that I'm wearing brown and green like a sensible, camouflaged zoologist. Is it still called zoology if you study people not animals?

I'll call the tall one Brown. His voice is deep which probably means that the pigeons are listening carefully. Pigeons can hear really low-pitched noises and even earthquakes and volcanoes which will be helpful in case any happen near Halham. They can be used to send messages to people. Maybe the grey pigeon with the damaged claw that I'm friends with will fly to my room tonight to report what Brown was saying.

The tree that hangs over from the farmer's field into ours drops little helicopters that twirl to the ground in autumn. It is wide and strong. Beside the tree, Brown grabs his friend. He looks around as if to check if anybody is spying, so I flatten my face to the ground. I stay as still as I can despite my legs wanting to twitch out of discomfort. Keeping very still is an important survival skill. It's hard though. My body doesn't like to stay in one position, it feels like it may get stuck and stay like that forever which is how statues are made.

After counting to one hundred, I raise my head slowly, glad that the grass here is uncut. Brown has pushed his friend against the tree. He is leaning down with his arm against the tree trunk, muscles taut like when he digs. Their faces are pushed together. They are kissing. The blond man tips his head back and Brown kisses the side of his neck, squashing into him close.

I know about kissing. Our study has a photobook with pictures of sculptures by Rodin. One is called 'The Kiss', two people wrapped up together as if nobody else on the planet is alive.

I feel funny lying on my front, like I'm pressing too hard into the ground, so roll over onto my back and stare at the passing clouds. I can usually make good stories from the shapes but not today. Today, all I see is the men kissing, the tightness of two clouds rolling towards each other as if they might become one. I push the back of my hand against my lips to see how it feels.

If things get too much, I have a trick to use. It doesn't have to be because of danger like aeroplanes or strangers or alarms. Sometimes it's because my feelings have turned up to ten out of ten and my head might explode if I can't escape. Human bodies are sixty per cent water. If you let your ears and eyes go fuzzy, all the water molecules in the body gather together as if you're drifting under water, hardly needing to breathe at all. If you get really good at it, you can float right out of your body and watch it down below you. It sounds scary but it's not. It's calm. It's zero out of ten feelings. It might be what it feels like to be dead.

It doesn't seem right to break the eavesdropping rule while the men are kissing. They make noises that aren't words. I let my body go soft as fleece on the ground. The water in my ears whooshes so I can't hear properly anymore. My heartbeats slow down with my breath. It's hard to pay attention as I float in my own water. Nothing from the outside can get in. It all seems so far away. It's comfortable and calm, a kind of being-nowhere feeling that I know can make the day go extra fast, as if someone moved the sun across the sky.

I don't notice that Brown and his friend are closer until it's too late.

'God, is she okay? She looks weird.' It's the blond one, standing over me and frowning with worry. 'Should we get her mother?'

I want to speak but the words won't come. How can I explain about trying to be a zoologist and floating in my own water? They mustn't call Mam, please no. I'm still half-floppy, unsure if I'm awake or dreaming when the bad thing happens: Brown bends down and scoops me right up. I feel unreal until he has me in his arms. With his top off, his warm torso presses against my shoulders, his arm against my arm. Skin to skin.

Energy rushes back into my body. I push against him to get away. It seems to take him by surprise and he lets me drop to the ground.

'What the hell, kid?'

I can't explain. I channel every bit of my battery into my legs to power home.

He'd touched me. Or I'd touched him. Either way, that was wrong. I don't know why exactly but that doesn't matter. It's something that should never happen, that's against the number one rule, and Mam will be so upset. My arm feels hot where it rested on his as if it's burnt. I need to get as far away as possible, back to the house. Stupid, stupid me. It was my fault, the skin thing. I went too near to the farm. I stayed there when I saw them even though I knew it was private, not for girls or scientists. Then I let myself float away instead of being careful.

I keep running even though my lungs burn and there's a metallic tang in my mouth. I don't know how long it takes to get poorly from touch. I've got to get back home before it happens. I'll be found out. Mam will cry and look at me in that same, dreadful way as when I picked up the floppy baby bird.

Bad, bad, bad girl.

4

IMOGEN

NOW

Imogen can't concentrate on the spreadsheet enough to make sense of the columns. Her eyes dart too quickly so that she loses her place. Although it frustrates her, she can't squeeze any more out of the day. Her sleep is poor and her aching limbs scold her for walking up the entire hill this morning.

She shuts off the computer and pulls the wifi wire out from the back of the tower. The damn thing is so old that it continues to hum in an attempt to stop itself overheating. Everything needs replacing but she knows the columns of numbers will tell her that's not a viable option, not without bringing in more income. She's tried to avoid it for as long as possible. Having outsiders around only increases the risk to Cate. But she can't hold out much longer.

The countdown to Cate's birthday ticks away on her internal clock. Twelve is such a more solid number than thirteen: twelve disciples; twelve months in a year; twelve pairs of ribs in a body. Divisible, solid, sensible twelve. What will happen to her solid, sensible girl this year as she tips into that cursed age as a teenager? Although it brings Cate one year closer to the safety of eighteen, there are three hundred and sixty-five days of the unlucky age up ahead to test them both.

Imogen rummages around for hand cream in her shoulder bag. The cocoa scent reminds her of circling moisturiser over her baby bump. She forces herself to take the time to cover each finger in turn with the cooling ointment. She recalls Cate's impossibly small fingers curling over hers almost immediately after birth. The instinct to hold onto each other was fierce. It had been painful at first to do what she must; painful in a different way to the aches her body endured – a kind of piercing inside her. She'd unfurled those beloved fingers from hers, wrapped Cate in the softest blanket she could find and vowed not to be so selfish as to put her own needs above her daughter's rights to own her body.

She dressed Cate in sleepsuits both day and night, stroking the soft cotton that housed her podgy arms and thighs. Her breasts had ached to feed her baby, leaking into pads and staining her clothes. But she knew she couldn't risk the skin-on-skin contact. It wouldn't be fair on Cate. Not for eighteen long years.

Imogen shakes her head and plants both feet firmly on the worn rug to ground herself. She often reflects on the need to act as her own parent. There can be no crumbling. She certainly never had an adult to depend on, although it took her many years to figure that out. People don't like to think badly of those they love. She didn't see what Father was because she didn't want to.

Selfish skewed into *well-intentioned.*

Stifling into *principled.*

Coercive into *confused.*

The very things people do to protect themselves and loved ones can be those that cause the most harm.

How does Cate perceive her as a mother? She almost

doesn't want to know. Parenting gets harder each year rather than easier, as if the rules change constantly in a game she can't afford to lose.

Time marches on, so they say. Right now, time feels like an invading army, ready to trample over her and her home. It threatens to turn their beautiful life together to sludge under its heavy boots, to knock her to the floor, carrying her daughter off on its shoulders, far away from the safety of their cocoon. She can almost hear it now: the thud of a thousand soldiers' feet. A different kind of invasion from those that Halham has endured in its ancient past but no less dangerous to their way of life.

Imogen drops her head then kneads the muscles at the base of her neck. How naïve she had been at eighteen, imagining that she could keep her daughter from the negative influences of the world by liberating her childhood from the demands of others. She won't let the plan fail nor let Cate down. How easy it would have been to repeat the family pattern – to turn Cate into a tiny version of herself to continue the tradition set by Imogen's grandmother, great-grandmother and who knows how many generations prior to that. Imogen's most important task as a mother is to prevent that. She must retain control and forge a new vision for them both.

Imogen had never known what it was like to not be serving others. She never had a life of her own or the freedom of games and exploration. Father drilled into her how work was of grave importance. That a good life was one of servitude and letting go of any focus on the self. Imagine telling that to a toddler! Yet it had all seemed normal to Imogen, all she'd ever known. When her mother tried to break them away from her husband's demands, Imogen had felt dread rather than relief. If she were no longer special, then what would become of her in her father's eyes? She can't recall exactly when her mother left but it simply never occurred to Imogen to go with her. She and

Father were two halves of a whole, incapable of surviving without the other.

It started before she was even born. One of Father's favourite stories was how it all began when Imogen was in utero. She plays back his calm voice in her mind.

'She showed she was special before we even met her,' he'd recite to the latest batch of people on their Rounds. The room was full, people of all ages crammed onto unmatching furniture in an unfamiliar place, the ceiling low with wooden beams, unusual smells from a hog farm almost overbearing to Imogen's small nose. Limp sandwiches and biscuits lay uneaten on a table in the corner. She clutched her father's trouser-leg, wishing she could climb up to dig her face into his armpit. Her stiff dress had short, puffed sleeves that dug into her arms. She'd outgrown it but Father hadn't noticed. A yellow ribbon was plaited across her head. Her hair was brushed one hundred times to fan out over each shoulder like a doll. Imogen had sipped blackcurrant juice from a carton on the journey. She needed the toilet but didn't tell anybody, not wanting to risk separation.

Even then, aged three or four, she noticed the way strangers looked at her. Their stares were hungry. The older people took their time – nodded and chatted with Father while keeping close watch of her. But the ones who were her parents' age or younger, those with little children of their own, they never waited. She could sense their urgency to get close to her.

An alarm sounds, shocking Imogen into the present. The second button down in the column of lights on the wall flashes amber: a post-box delivery. It's rare for letters to arrive.

Imogen tries to maintain a normal speed out of the house down to the letter box but her smoothness has gone. Her nerves fire an alarm long after the electrical one has hushed. She feels unsettled, as if something she has been dreading may have finally started. The strange thing is that this familiar sensation is not one hundred per cent negative. It's as though she has clutched onto a tiny element of hope; one per cent of her believes there is still goodness out in the world and that it will somehow find its way into their lives. As Imogen unlocks the letter box and extracts the handwritten letter, a flash of movement catches her eye. It's Cate. Running as fast as if her life depended on it.

5
____

CATE

As I run closer to the house, I see Mam outside, wide-eyed. I want to stop and find a way to explain that will change the way her face looks but I'm desperate to be inside. To show my plan, I point to the door and make the final sprint. In the hallway, I bend forward panting, my hands on my thighs to hold me up.

Mam rushes in then locks the door behind her. She understands that sometimes we need to keep the world out. We are little pigs in our house made of glass. Its walls protect us.

Please, please let it be enough to block the big bad wolf of what happened, who howls right outside saying, "Let me in".

'What on earth is wrong?'

Bad girl, bad touch, bad things to follow.

It scares me that Mam doesn't look right. Her face is screwed up, her voice higher pitched, her agitated feet shuffle back and forth as if she wants to grab hold of me but can't. She hasn't been like this for so long. I must make it better.

Half-truth isn't the same as a lie. Mam knows when I lie. What part can I tell her? *Think, think, breathe.*

'The farmer's helpers, I saw them, I didn't mean to.' I do my best to blow my breath in a straight line to get back control. My legs feel wobbly. I try to turn them to stone.

'Did they get near to you? What did they do? Did they hurt you?'

Come on, Cate. Only think of the part of the story you can tell. The tree, Brown's arm, his leaning into the man.

'No, I saw them, the helpers, down the field. I saw them doing kissing.'

Kissing might be the very worst kind of touch but it wasn't me, so at least that part can't hurt us, can it? Mam's shoulders drop down from high alert into neutral. She tips her head back and does a sigh that's so long I wonder how she had that much air inside her. I clench my teeth.

'Those boys! Cate, that's not for you to spy on. Did they see you?'

The best way to tell a lie is to make the new scene as real as possible in your mind. The story becomes a new memory, like you are watching back what happened. I move Brown to the other side of the field. The oak tree becomes a linden tree with bright love-heart leaves. The men shrink smaller now I've pushed them so far away, their outlines hazy with distance. I can hear the tractor's rumble not their strange moans. I don't use my extra eye or lie down on the grass. Instead, in this version, I turn immediately to run home like a good girl. My skin feels clean and perfect.

'I couldn't see very well from across the field but I think they were kissing, like the Rodin statue. I didn't want to be eavesdropping.' *Don't let her know about the sounds, she'll know how close you were.* 'Well, I couldn't hear anything over the tractor so I mean I didn't want to be eyesdropping.'

It comes out muddled but Mam's arms are still loose at her sides instead of her hands clinging on to one another.

'They didn't see me. They kissed and then Brown went

back to the tractor.' I don't know why I added that ending. It felt weird to leave the story with them kissing, as if they'll never stop, as if it's still going on now and I won't be able to go back to the field where I left my magnifying glass behind in the rush.

Mam's eyes narrow just a teeny bit. Uh-oh.

'Brown? Is that what you've called him?'

I shouldn't have used my name for him. I can't keep the images out any longer. His messy hair that drops across his face, his biceps leaning on the tree, the warmth of his chest. I feel my face burning. Mam is going to figure out that he picked me up and held my body against his. It's my fault. She'll get so upset that everything will fall apart again.

I'm sobbing before I can tell myself any other kind of story. It pours from my eyes, my nose, wet and snotty all over.

'Oh baby.' Mam's voice is gentle. She puts her hand on the sleeve of my T-shirt, close to where Brown touched me. 'You like him! I forget how grown up you are now. He's a handsome boy, I guess.' She isn't cross. I'm unsure why. Her danger dial has turned lower. I want to stay like this, her hand warm through the cotton of my clothes but I'm scared that Brown's touch might contaminate her so I step back.

Mam pulls herself up straight. She's holding something white in her left hand; her index finger taps the outside of it. 'I know it hurts but it's better this way. He likes boys. That means he's not interested in... girls.' She looks relieved.

I know what she means. She means he wouldn't like to kiss me, even if I were a grown woman. Nobody ever will. I already knew that, but today it makes me feel as if a cow has rammed into my stomach, sending me crashing into the ground, broken and ugly. I rub the back of my hand wishing I could erase the feeling of it against my lips. What kind of disgusting girl tries to kiss herself?

I'm exhausted. I'd like to burrow into the earth and hide

with the moles. The wet, dark soil would be a haven with night-time creatures to keep me company. Nobody would see us in the dark. We'd dig and dig down into the quiet warmth of the earth.

'Can I go to my room?' I mustn't hint that I don't feel well: that always sets off Mam's worry and questions. 'I'm tired. From the science, and the running.'

'Why don't you have a little rest? I'll be up shortly.' Mam looks as if she has more to say. I want to escape before she reaches down into my hidey-hole and realises that I haven't told her everything. 'You know you can tell me if anything new or strange happens in your body? Any kinds of pain or cramps, or any bleeding?'

Is that what happens after you've been touched? Pain and blood?

I hum my agreement so my fear can't seep out through my open mouth, then I run up to the safety of my bedroom. I check my arms and torso for marks or a rash but my skin looks the same as usual. I sniff myself to see if I smell different. I check my eyeballs in the mirror for any change of colour. There's no sign of blood yet anywhere.

I turn sideways and look at my reflection. The material of my T-shirt no longer lies flat against my chest. Two little bumps push at the material. I'm not sure how long they've been there. I keep my arms down so I don't see the hairs under my armpits. I want to be smooth all over again, like a doll. My stomach churns but I've had that before, it's what happens when my guts twist into a double knot.

I flop onto the bed. Brown picked me up but it was over so fast, perhaps I've avoided the side effects? Or maybe they take a long time to show? I remember back when some cattle caught a disease that made them thinner and thinner until their own legs couldn't hold them.

Mam asked Farmer Grove if he was going to call the vet. He'd said there was no point – nothing could be done except to watch and wait for the inevitable.

Mam knocks on the door then opens it before I can reply. I reset my face to zero out of ten, even though underneath it feels more like a nine. She leans against the door-frame, keeping her distance. Half her body is out of view and I can't help but wonder what was in her hand earlier that was so important she didn't put it down.

I hide from her. She hides from me. I don't like it this way.

'You know we only need each other to be happy.' It's one of Mam's sayings. It's usually soothing to hear but today it's as if she's not talking to me. Her eyes have that glazed look that doesn't quite meet mine. It's like she's looking right through me to another place or time. All I want is for Mam to be happy but I don't think being with me is always enough for her. Not when I get things wrong.

Mam half-closes her eyes like a cat kiss. She's not too upset with me. I'll have a chance to repair things. I must get it back to how it was between us. I'll make a list in my head of all our happiest times to see what would work best. She never needs to know what happened with Brown today. Mam shuts the door and I stay still until I hear her close the study door downstairs.

I need to keep careful watch over my body and hide any symptoms that could give anything away. I can hide pains but not blood. I'll never be so selfish again. Me and Mam. Mam and me. I've got to make it enough for her. That's all we need.

I don't allow a different thought to find a place inside my head. I squash it and squeeze it until it disappears altogether.

6

IMOGEN

NOW

The events of this afternoon have taken their toll. Imogen closes the blinds in her study and nestles onto her reading chair with her feet tucked under her. Fatigue pulls at her, heavy and unforgiving. Her little girl's first crush – a heartbreak at distance. She should have thought about the impact of having young men around Cate. How can she stop her daughter becoming restless or distracted at this age? The problem with teenagers is they have one foot in the future while their emotional balance reverts back to toddler level. She mustn't let Cate's neediness attach itself elsewhere. How do you keep a songbird safe if you let it out of its cage?

The silence of late evening is a balm. Imogen doubts she could ever tolerate the noisy chaos of town life again. If only her daughter could appreciate what she's protected from.

Cate's flushed face at the recollection of the young farmer stirs a visceral memory in Imogen. Fifteen years ago, her own body had given away her carefully monitored emotions. Zach always had the ability to break through her walls.

Imogen unfolds the envelope that has been in her back

pocket all evening. She forced herself to complete her chores without taking it out. Self-control is key to avoiding mistakes. It has a postmark from Cornwall. It's been so long since Imogen last left Halham and its surrounds that the specifics of the sea now seem unreal; the tang of salted air, hot sand underfoot, uninterrupted horizon.

Of all the things she misses, packed tightly into lockboxes of her past, those few trips to the North Wales coast with Zach are the most precious. The out-of-season greyness and desolation created the ideal location for them to be together away from Imogen's responsibilities and Father's eye.

After craving the freedom of childhood for so long, Zach had turned her yearning in the opposite direction. She couldn't wait to become an adult, to make her own life with him. But they never got the chance. It makes sense that he travelled as far as he could away from this place, down to the foot of the country. She begged him to leave but could just as easily have begged him to stay: a fork in the road that dictated everything about the last thirteen years and beyond.

The left-leaning slant of the handwriting is familiar to her despite the years that have passed. She presses the sharp edge of the envelope into the pad of her thumb.

Stay alert. Don't weaken.

'Zach.' Imogen whispers his name. It would be a lie to say she never thought about him. When her guard was down as she settled to sleep or sat in the backyard with a cider watching the sunset, one scene would play from their time together before it all crashed apart: Zach tilting her chin up toward him. That was all. But it was the first time in her life that somebody touched her without a desire to take something from her for themselves. He saw who she was rather than what she was.

They'd met when they were both sixteen. Imogen had been

at the lakeside sketching designs in her notepad for a tattoo that she'd never get. It was part of her plan to reclaim her body at eighteen. The problem was that the images in her mind never translated onto the page. Her hand was awkward and quick to ache. She tried to replicate the swirls that adorned her grandmother's magnifying glass with the addition of thorns. The design was to encircle her upper arm.

Imogen had seen Zach a couple of times at that spot. Dark hair that he flicked in different directions, khaki shorts against tanned legs, a gracefulness as he ran or cycled that she would never possess, as if he were made for movement.

'Is it barbed wire?' he asked, leaning his bike against the back of the bench.

Imogen felt her mouth dry up, unsure if he was mocking her yet pleased that the design projected what she wanted it to: keep out. She was used to playing a part by then, so forced her voice to come out clear and confident. 'It's for my tattoo.'

Zach glanced up at her before focusing back on the drawing. His eyes were hazel, quite different from the blue of her family. Imogen couldn't yet tell if he had an agenda, whether this was a warm-up for asking her about the Rounds or to come and visit a family member. It had happened several times when she thought she was starting to make a friend.

'Can I have a go?' He nodded towards her notepad. 'Think I've got an idea.'

His question was so unexpected that Imogen passed her pad and pencil over without argument. He was offering to help her. Not asking for something.

She watched as he curled his body over the page. He used his left hand to sketch in fast, gentle strokes, his lips slightly parted as he concentrated. He made small sounds of satisfaction to himself. Somehow, the shading he did with ease brought the image to life as if it stood off the page. The thorns were ready to spike into anyone's fingers who touched without permission. The curls of each link in the chain had the sheen of silver like the original magnifying glass handle.

When he finished, he turned the page towards Imogen. 'You'd look great with this.' He cocked his head to the side with a slow smile that made her believe that everything was about to change.

He stood, signed the page with a 'Z' and got back on his bike. Imogen realised she hadn't said thank you or praised his drawing, suddenly panicked that the best moment of her life was over.

The beautiful boy called back over his shoulder as he set off. 'I'm Zach. See you tomorrow?'

She already knew the answer. Father, the Rounds, sixteen years of service – none had as much power over her as Zach's invitation – expectation – that they meet again. He didn't know who she was or what she could do. He wanted to see her anyway.

Imogen had wandered home in a daze, the bridge from childhood to adulthood now clear to her.

Imogen holds the letter to her chest, as if that could bring the writer's hand closer to her, through time and distance. The impossibility of reliving those years, of making different choices, is so cruel that she has preferred the safety of numbness. Now her emotions threaten to ram the barricade that she had so carefully constructed.

It's after midnight, the start of a new day. Cate is now thirteen and it doesn't seem coincidence that here is a letter from Imogen's past to signal the start of what may be her year of bad luck. Imogen knows she should tear it into a hundred pieces or write "return to sender" to give Zach the impression she left long ago. It's as though her fingers make the choice for her, pulling at the back of the envelope with that faint, absurd hope of rectifying a dreadful wrong.

> *Dear Imogen*
>
> *How did we get to the age of thirty? Last time we actually saw each other we'd only just become adults. I couldn't think what I wanted to do for my birthday and planned a trip north on the 14th before realising it meant I'd be so close to you. I'll stop off at Halham on the way. I hope you let me in.*
>
> *Yours,*
> *Zach*

The note contains so few words but Imogen picks them apart to try to decipher Zach's mood, intentions, how he may have changed, what it would be like to see each other again. That's out of the question of course, she can't risk the disruption to Cate's life. But see how he writes "yours". Not "yours sincerely" or "from" but "yours" as if he still belongs to her. He hopes she'll let him in. Into the house? Into her life? Or into her secrets? Imogen knows her overthinking is futile but it's preferable to pick at words than at memories.

The house has cooled. Imogen shivers as the sweat from her first flushed reading starts to evaporate. She pulls a huge woollen sweater over her shoulders. The weight of it is a comfort. The heavy sleeves over her shoulders feel like two arms wrapped around her. She throws off the damned thing and decides to warm up by exercise instead.

Imogen strides fast enough to burn the backs of her legs as she makes her way down towards the row of stone cottages. Cloud cover prevents her from seeing the stars, adding to a sense of suffocation. When has Halham ever seemed so small? Her hands shake a little as she reaches The Blacksmith's Cottage and unlocks the door, groping her way around in the darkness to find the chair that sits beneath the window of the living room. Heavy velvet drapes keep out the light. This is where she comes to speak with Father, away from Cate, away from her everyday life so as not to taint her home with such weakness. It doesn't matter that Father can't reply, in fact that's the only reason she can be honest with him in a way that was impossible as a child or young woman.

'It's Zach. He's written to say he wishes to visit.' Saying it out loud helps Imogen to feel more solid again. Just a problem to be dealt with, head over heart. 'He's passing by here anyway, not a special trip so it won't be too much of a problem if I don't let him in.' She doesn't let anyone in. Deliveries are carefully managed with the outdoor food store used as a drop-off point so there's no need for anyone to come to her door. Electric gates with high-tech video surveillance give her total control over who has access.

Over the years, people have learned not to bother. She hasn't responded to old acquaintances or neighbouring farmers for over a decade. The glass panes she selected that give such amazing views at the back of the house are half-silvered mirror glass, reflective from the outside. She can't help but imagine Zach peering into the kitchen and seeing only himself.

'The thing is, back then when Zach... when he...' She raises her arm, unable to put the act into words even now. 'It wasn't what it seemed. He had the wrong information. I didn't lie to him, I never did, but he got the wrong end of the stick and I didn't correct it when I should have.'

Imogen hangs her head down. This is the only place where she allows herself to cry. 'I'm sorry. What happened was my fault; I could have prevented it. I never told Zach afterwards that it was my fault. I only told him to get far away to avoid the repercussions.'

She has said sorry to Father many, many times. But she's never said sorry to Zach. In fact, he doesn't know she has anything to be sorry about. He has spent the last thirteen years thinking he committed a dreadful crime to protect her.

7

CATE

Today's lesson is all about dandelions. Mam leans back on her elbows in the field with her ankles crossed over. I try to copy but it feels uncomfortable after a couple of minutes so I flip over to lie on my stomach and rest my head in my palms placed over each. If I can't do the same as Mam, I like to try to do the opposite. That way we're mirror twins.

'A long time ago, before foolish people started to call dandelions a weed, they were appreciated. The Egyptians, Romans, Greeks and Chinese knew about how special they were for healing.' She runs her finger along the jagged edges of a dandelion leaf without pulling it from the ground. 'There are more vitamins in here than in some of our vegetables. They're also good for the grass and the bees.'

It's the time of year when there are some dandelions that are still yellow and others that have changed to white clouds. So even the dandelions are same-but-different like me and Mam.

'Can we blow them now?' I'm trying to pay attention because I love it when Mam is excited about what she teaches me but I'm itching to make the magic happen. The natural world has all the answers in it. You just need to know where to look and how to ask it.

'Wait a minute, Cate. This is important. Did you know many people pull all their dandelions up and try to get rid of them? But it's not so simple! These plants are full of special powers and the earth knows that it needs them. So, they can grow just about anywhere. The roots grow far underground and each part of the root can grow a new dandelion, even in places that look stony or full of man-made materials.'

We both stare at the white dandelion. It doesn't look like it's strong and determined: the fuzzy parts are so soft and floaty. It's hard to understand why anyone wouldn't like to have such beautiful flowers in their garden or across their fields. But Mam says that Outsiders think peculiar things and then they catch one another's ideas like a virus, until everyone does the same thing without thinking for themselves.

'It's sad that people would rip them out. Maybe they don't realise they're magic?'

Mam sighs. 'People don't always know what's good for them, especially when they lose the old ways. Not everything has to be packaged in plastic and bought in a shop or pharmacy.'

I wish I had interesting facts to tell Mam. Everything I learn comes from her so there's nothing useful I can add unless I've seen something with my own eyes. I suppose she learnt all her lessons from Grandfather. Who will I have to teach?

I realise I've been lost in a thread of thought while Mam was still talking. It's selfish not to pay attention. I try to look like I've been listening all along.

'We used to call them puff balls when I was little. I didn't realise that they were the same thing as the yellow dandelions. They look so different, don't they – but really, they're the same flower at a different stage.'

'Did you used to be called something else, before you were Imogen?'

Mam sits up. 'What a funny question! No, I've always been Imogen.' She looks away for just one second that makes me think there's a name she's not telling me about. 'And you've always been Cate, even before you were born. I decided on Catelyn and I took one look at you once you were born and I knew it was just right.

'I'm Catelyn? More than just Cate?'

Mam laughs. 'It's the same name; the shorter version suits you.'

It's not the same name. That's a strange thing to say. It is a new name that sounds and feels totally different. I sit up and the world spins a little bit because I did it too fast. Mam says that's something to do with inside your ears but I think it might be when you catch the earth turning round. My name is more than Cate but Mam never thought to tell me that. I wonder what else she hasn't told me?

I mustn't ruin things. The dandelion spell will help.

'Can we blow now? One each?' I rub my hand over the delicate fuzz of the flower, being careful not to damage it.

I sit opposite Mam so we are facing each other with our legs crossed. Maybe this is what I'll look like with a few lines on my face, a woman's figure, hands that need to be rubbed in lotion every day.

'Ready to make a wish? One, two, three!'

We blow one dandelion each and send their baby seeds floating across the field. Just two flowers could become hundreds more. My wish is that me and Mam can stay happy together forever. I think that's her wish too which makes it double-strength and more powerful.

I lean back on my elbows as the dandelion seeds dance in the breeze towards Hart Hill. They are free to go where they like. I blink a message to them to let me know what they see from up there so I can paint it in my mind. I feel like I'm choking on a stone so I need to think about something else before I spoil everything. My birds will help.

'I learnt a new birdsong. Do you want to hear?'

Mam gave me a special black machine that records sounds when you press a red button. You can listen to the same part again and again while you copy the music. 'I recorded the blackbird. I can't do it by whistling, that's too hard. I'll have to sing it.'

'I'll close my eyes to pay close attention. Maybe you'll fool the birds around us that there's a blackbird right here!'

I like that we both have our eyes shut. I turn my bottom into a fluffy tail, my mouth into a bright yellow beak. The breeze blows the feathers of my wings. I start to sing. I've only learnt a few lines. I do the best I can even though I know it doesn't sound the same as the real bird. Sometimes it's good to have things to copy when you don't know what to do or say yourself.

Mam picks up on the three lines and tries to join in with the tune. She's really terrible at it.

'That's not quite right, Mam.'

I try not to laugh but Mam giggles first and that sets me off. We both have our eyes open now. She starts to whistle, flapping her elbows to the side. She can't keep going because she's laughing too much and that makes me laugh even more until my eyes water. I jump up and run around Mam being a female blackbird who loves the male's song. She chases after me, whooping in a way that doesn't sound like any bird at all but it doesn't matter. The dandelions have done their spell and nothing can ever break it.

8

IMOGEN

AGE 4

The nursing home was called The Old Elm Tree and smelled like rotten vegetables. Imogen sat on Father's lap and played with his tie. He had his blue suit on. There was a tickly feeling from Father's moustache as he whispered into her ear. 'Can you count the people like a big girl?'

Easy-peasy. One, two, three, four people in big chairs and a smiling lady in a nurse's outfit equals five. She held up her hand to show five fingers but didn't want to talk in front of everyone.

'Clever girl! Now, you know what to do. One person at a time. Who do you think needs you the most? Take your time to choose.'

Imogen kept hold of Father's tie but moved her head slowly from one side of the room to the other. The first lady looked cuddly without any teeth. Maybe she ate custard for breakfast which would be very nice.

Next to her was a man in a wheelchair. He seemed to have fallen asleep. His glasses were wonky but nobody put them back on straight, not even the nurse.

Next was a lady who was small enough to be friends with

Imogen. She was so old that time had started to go backwards to shrink her back to nursery size.

The last lady looked cross and talked to herself.

Imogen pointed to the small lady who beamed back. That made Imogen feel nice. She knew without looking that Father was smiling too.

The nurse had blonde hair tied up on the top of her head with bits sticking out like a pineapple. She put her arm on Imogen and walked her over to the small lady. Imogen did a secret sniff. She couldn't smell pineapple on the nurse but a different type of perfume that was a bit like vanilla ice cream. Everybody went quiet. Even the cross, horrible lady. They all watched her. This was an important part of the Rounds. Imogen glanced back at Father who nodded his head. That meant *good girl, carry on.*

The old lady reached out her hand. It had too much skin. Her fingers shook like one of Imogen's toys with batteries in. She had long nails that were a bit yellow. She wore a diamond ring like a princess. Maybe that was what she used to be a long, long time ago. Imogen looked around the room and felt a bit sorry for the old princess. One day she might disappear altogether and only the nurse would notice.

Father started to talk about faith and bonds and healing. Imogen watched the vanilla nurse who looked at Father with her mouth open and her eyebrows up. The nurse's cheeks turned red. She held her arms up to her chest as if she was holding flowers on a wedding day. Everybody wanted to marry Father even though he was already married. Even Imogen.

'And now I ask for quiet while Immy does her special work. If all of us believe, it will be so.'

Imogen took the old lady's hand into both of hers. The lady smiled and watched her. She was full of germs that made her poorly. Imogen could see the green germs under the lady's skin.

They floated in the white bits of her eyeballs, dripped down her mouth, moved along the line of her veins on the back of her hands. Imogen pressed her finger on the blue-green line that ran from one finger down to the lady's wrist. That's where the bad blood was. The germs rushed towards her touch. The man in the next chair woke up and started to cry out so the nurse gave him a tablet and stroked his head.

Imogen closed her eyes and waited for the tingling. She knew everybody was staring at her, waiting. She needed to call all the germs to come to her through the old lady's skin. Imogen wriggled her thumb a little bit to make a warm patch. She felt the tingling first in her hands. Then it spread over her body like the pins and needles that come if you wear a rubber band around your wrist for too long. Imogen had to try very hard now. She breathed fast to heave the germs out of the lady. Faster and faster. Her head was thumping, her hands tingled, her legs turned to jelly. The old lady's hand was getting hot inside hers as the germs flooded out of her blood and into the skin on Imogen's thumb. She sucked more and more of the badness out. It was hot and stingy in her hands, travelling up her arms and into her belly. *Hold on, keep going, don't let go yet.* Father told everyone it was okay and that Imogen was nearly finished then bam! She turned to cooked spaghetti and her body flopped onto the floor.

She was a good girl. She was special. Everyone in the room knew it now.

The next part was nice. A drink of real Ribena with a straw which the nurse made extra strong because sugar is good for energy. A blue lollipop. Father's knee and a hug. Imogen was so tired. She'd been such a good girl helping the lady. She wanted to curl up in the car and sleep but she knew there was more work to be done. The vanilla nurse stroked her hair and called her *sweetheart* and a *little gem.* Father placed his hand on the pretty nurse's arm for a little too long, so Imogen told him she was ready for the next patient.

The grumpy lady pointed to Imogen and said, 'Come here,' her finger bent like a witch. Her eyes didn't look right. They were covered with white. Imogen wondered how the witch lady knew where she was. Perhaps she smelled her. Imogen didn't want to go near her but she needed to get the nurse away from Father. The vanilla nurse walked over with her.

'Behave yourself, Iris, this is the special girl I was telling you about. She might be able to help with your eyes. Or your memory. Let's see, shall we?'

Iris made a strange sound in the back of her throat. Imogen felt her heart move out of place, up from her chest into her mouth. She wrapped her fingers around the witch's wrist rather than holding her hand. Iris's blood was fast and made Imogen's ear roar with the sound of it deep inside. There was a little drum in there. Father told her that. Iris's blood made the drum in her ear beat fast and loud. Imogen wanted to step back but Father was looking over, waiting for her to do her work. Imogen formed her lips into a smile and held her breath. Iris dug her long, pointed nails into the back of Imogen's hand.

'Get this little devil away from me! Get away!' the scary woman shrieked and tried to push Imogen over but collapsed back into her chair. The vanilla nurse stood between them and Father grabbed Imogen, pulling her through the air as if she was flying. Her hand was bleeding. Father carried her out of the room, howling and hot. At the front of the building, he pulled the door shut, placed Imogen onto a stone wall and wrapped her bleeding hand with his tie.

'I'm sorry. She wasn't the right one. I should have noticed that you didn't choose her. I let it go too fast.'

The vanilla nurse came out, tearful with bright red cheeks. She talked fast and low with Father. Imogen heard her say *dementia* and *medication.* She wanted Father to say *bad* and *wrong* and *poor Imogen,* but instead he turned his back to her. Father hugged the vanilla nurse who laid her head on his shoulder as if she was his little girl.

It was all the vanilla nurse's fault. She made the witch lady hurt Imogen so she could try to steal Father.

'My hand hurts, I want to go home!'

Father sighed and whispered more things to the nurse, then picked Imogen up and carried her to the car.

'All in a day's work,' he said, as if it didn't matter at all that Imogen's hand and heart stung.

He strapped her into the car seat and made a little pillow from a jumper for her to rest her hand on.

'Let's go home and get you to bed. We can come back to the other two next week.'

Imogen didn't reply. She needed to make sure Father loved her the best. He said they don't need anybody else. Mother spent weekends with her cousin who lived in the city. They didn't mind. She got in the way and never helped with the Rounds.

Imogen didn't cry or fuss again on the way home even though she knew her body would ache later. She had to be sure that the green germs didn't get into the scratches on her hand. She rolled down the window and tried to shoo them out into the fields but they didn't want to leave her body. If she had thought at the time, she could have sent the germs flying up the nurse's nostrils, into her ears and under her fingernails. Perhaps she could try next week.

'I love you,' she called from the back seat.

'Love you too, Immy. You're a good girl.'

Imogen watched the last few green germs move under the skin on the inside of her wrist then bob along the blue line of her blood up her arms, towards her heart.

9

———

CATE

The bad thing is happening. There are parts of my insides coming out in small chunks. When I went to the toilet there was a dab of bright red blood in my pants. Mam warned me about blood and pain. The blood isn't liquid like when you cut your finger and lift the cotton wool ball to watch the next red drip run down. It's gloopy and dark. I tried to soak it all up with tissue but more came. I've got to hide it so she doesn't find out about Brown holding me. But what if the bleeding never stops until all the blood in my body has drained out? I'll be dried out and flat. Mam will fold me over and over then lock my paper body in the filing cabinet.

I try to push the image away by keeping busy in the garden. The toilet paper screwed up in my underwear feels scratchy and I'm worried it will move or fall out. I kneel down to keep the pain and blood and toilet roll in place. The most important thing is to be okay when Mam arrives.

I can't get rid of the yucky feeling inside me as the invisible woodlice crawl under my skin. Sometimes they fall onto their backs and get trapped against my veins, their little legs frantically pushing against the under-skin of my arms and legs.

It's so itchy and horrible that I want to grab the gardening scissors and slice along each limb so the woodlice can escape. They'd scuttle off to a dark place covered in lumps of my flesh.

That's not the kind of thing that would help Mam feel better. It's not the kind of thing that a good girl does.

Mam pushes the wheelbarrow over towards me at the side of the vegetable plot. She's wearing her denim dungarees with the peach shirt beneath. Good news! These are the clothes that she wears on her most active days so I know she's not too stuck in the pictures of her mind. Her face doesn't match the outfit yet. It's too stiff like she's wearing her mask of okayness, the same as me.

'What are you up to?'

Mam smiles but she looks from one of my eyes to the other which is what she does when she's trying to see inside my head. In case she can, I make sure that at the front of my mind are images of thousands of daisies dancing in a field. But that reminds me of crouching low near to Brown and his friend so I quickly switch that to picturing a beautiful spider web that covers my brain, dripping with dew, hiding my thoughts.

'I was thinking about all my favourite things.'

It's not totally a lie because that was what I'd planned to do but not got round to yet. Mam doesn't take anything out of the wheelbarrow so I know it was an excuse to come out to see me. It feels good to sit close. The woodlice inside me settle to sleep. I let my mind take a wander so I can think of something to say to Mam that will show I'm fine.

'You know that spider web in French is *toile*. It means lots of other things too, like cloth and the canvas you paint on, and a sail.'

Mam likes it when I talk about sensible things like words. She has the same kind of brain as mine that easily sees the links between things so jumps from one thing to another. In fact, it's probably a bit like a web – a huge, beautiful pattern of thoughts where each follows multiple lines. She laughs which loosens the tightness in her forehead, moving those frown lines to the side of her eyes. I can never guess which things I say make things better or worse.

'I take it you've been looking up your favourite French words in the dictionary again.'

'Yes, and toile is also the curtain that they have in a theatre like the pictures you showed me from London. The French say "*derrière la toile*" for "behind the curtain" which is where the actors wait to do a show, isn't it?' I wonder what it would feel like to watch a play on a big stage. To stare as the curtains open and the actors speak lines as if they are thoughts that just popped into their heads.

'Yes, huge curtains that open and close for different parts of the play so that the new scene can be set up.'

I imagine theatres in the olden days when there was Shakespeare but I'm pretty sure they still exist. We don't talk about outside the village. The way Mam is looking past me makes me think she's been to a theatre and she's revisiting right now. I want to ask but I daren't spoil the mood. She's away from me when I want her to stay close. Mam has the choice to travel in her mind because she has places to return to. I've never been anywhere. I'm stuck in sameness.

I start to feel warm. My cheeks are hot to the touch and I know if I glance down, I'll see the flush of a rash over my chest – little red islands on a white map of skin. The woodlice start to stir again. Or it could be millipedes by the feel of thousands of tiny legs moving in unison.

'How do the actors know where to stand or when it's their turn to talk or what to say?'

Mam rolls back off her heels to sit on the grass. 'Well, the script tells them what to say, like the ones we looked at. But there is a person in charge called the director who decides where people are placed on the stage and how to present the scenes.'

Wouldn't it be wonderful to have a script now so I knew what to say and I also knew what Mam would say back?

'Can the actors ever change the words to their own?'

Mam gets the trowel from behind her and starts to mark out where she's going to dig. I'll lose her attention once the task absorbs her.

'No, it's very important to say the lines exactly right. Can you move along a little so I can reach that corner, Cate?'

So, the audience goes to watch people who they know are not real, saying things they don't mean. Everybody is pretending.

Wriggle, writhe go the little furry legs beneath my skin.

It's not always that easy to tell fact from fiction even if it's something I've learnt from Mam. She tells me so many stories that I'm not always certain if we are studying history or literature. There are in-between people. They are not quite fact and not quite fiction, like the Pied Piper of Hamelin who stole the children from a village or the Little Match Girl who had beautiful visions before she froze to death.

I do my best to be an actor. I make my face neutral and I don't move my body but it's no good. It feels too horrible on the inside.

Mam puts down the trowel and turns to me. 'What's the matter? I can see your brain working away there.'

I knew she could see in. I forgot to focus on the spider web behind my eyes. I dip my head down in shame.

'Am I real, Mam?'

She doesn't answer. I don't have a script but sometimes it does feel as if a director has told me what to do or say. I copy what I can from Mam although it never looks or sounds the same. I'm trying to learn how to be a human. Halham feels like a stage. Mam is always watching me, maybe others are too, like it's a show or a practice for real life? Why isn't my life normal like Mam's was when she was little, or the holidaymakers, or the people she teaches me about in history? I don't have friends or any other family. Nobody talks to me except Mam.

When I glance up, Mam is crying into her hands. I don't know if that means she's sad that I'm real or sad that I'm not.

10

____

IMOGEN

AGE 19

Imogen watched her baby doze under the shade of an oak tree.

She had thought when she was a child that she knew what fatigue was. The relentless travel and performance of the Rounds was tiring but absolutely nothing compared to caring for an infant by herself.

She had expected the rules of parenting to be hardwired. Growing up surrounded by farms and Father's speeches about the self-sufficiency of nature had created a belief that she'd be directed by her genes once the baby arrived. In reality, she was missing those primal instincts. Imogen felt less suited to the practicalities of motherhood than the small-brained sheep in the next field.

Her love for Cate was deep and animalistic even though she was unsure what to do with it other than stare at her baby's sleeping face. She recalled the sound cows made when parted from their calves; a deep, painful lowing that could last for weeks. Such cruelty in separation. She vowed never to be further away from Cate than shouting distance. But that didn't help her know what to do while they were close.

The baby preferred to be outdoors. She leant forwards on

the grass and sunk her face into flowers as if they were food. Cate held her podgy fingers in the air and cooed at curious birds. In the giddiness of sleep deprivation, Imogen wondered if the birds were drawn to her daughter. Blackbirds and round-bellied robins sang to her from nearby branches. Imogen was certain they'd never been so vocal before.

'What are they saying, Cate?'

Cate babbled her excitement; a secret language for her friends. Imogen stopped herself from shooing the pests away.

'Don't you eat my seeds, you little buggers.'

Cate giggled her encouragement to them. A hopping wren side-eyed Imogen and stayed close to her daughter who bounced along with it. Imogen recalled Father saying that perhaps dinosaurs had been covered in feathers. She imagined the wren now stripped of its plumage; a tiny dinosaur in plain sight. The air thickened making it hard to breathe.

Imogen stilled each part of her body in turn until she solidified. She placed feathers back onto the birds and dug her nails into the warm earth.

Imogen needed to mark out the ground to create a vegetable patch for them both. Behind it, the outline of the house that would be constructed shortly looked more like ruins from the past than plans for the future. Where the old shed had been pulled down, poles and tape delineated the ground level of their new home.

What would the builders find as they dug into the earth to prepare the ground? Hundreds of years of Halham history would be excavated and scooped into a skip by unthinking machines as if they had never existed.

It was essential that the vegetable patch lay in front of their new home just as it should. But everything took so much longer with a baby to care for.

More than that, Imogen's own mind was becoming her

enemy. She knew what would happen as soon as she turned her back to Cate to focus on marking out the ground. She pushed a bright peg into the soil as hard as she could. Her fingers throbbed. Pain pushed up her arm into her shoulder blade. Even that wasn't enough to stop the images returning.

Imogen imagined the brown wren tilting its head as soon as she turned her back. It hopped closer to Cate who held out her arm in delight, then fluttered up to land on her shoulder, its sharp beak three centimetres from her daughter's hazel eyes, a chirp of satisfaction as it pulled its head back, ready to pierce a soft cornea.

She glanced behind her. Cate was busy refilling a cup with water from the washing up bowl next to her, then pouring it onto the grass. Imogen turned back to continue her task. She could hear birds call and sing, camouflaged in the trees. *Don't be so stupid. Get this done. She's fine.* Imogen measured along the width of the vegetable patch with her mother's old sewing tape.

The images returned in her mind's eye. She could picture a cloud of birds descending on the baby. They swarmed around the straps of her clothes to lift her into the air, far away from Imogen, as if she'd never become a mother at all.

Imogen spun around and scooped up her daughter around her middle and carried her under her arm, the cold metal buckle of Cate's dungarees pressing into her side like a weapon.

'Time for bed. An early night. Mummy is so tired.'

It would all be different when the new house was finished; everything would be fresh and new, only for them. The fog would lift.

She had been right to ignore her urges to hold Cate since she was a baby. It wasn't her daughter's role to suck out her sadness or settle the waves of dread and anxiety that parenting elicited. She'd never feel obligated to trade her freedom for strangers' health. There was no gift unless it was channelled.

In Imogen's childhood bedroom, Cate snored lightly in the single bed nearest the window. It was cracked open to allow her to hear the sounds that soothed her to sleep. Imogen crawled into the other single bed. She'd never managed to move to Father's old study or her parents' bedroom. It was better to be here with Cate than imagining all the ways in which she could be harmed. She could keep a close eye on any potential dangers. Imogen rolled over to face the mirrored wardrobe and stared at her own reflection.

11
———

CATE

There's a strange energy from Mam today. If it was a colour it would be bright orange – halfway between sunshine yellow and fire red. That's better than her grey days but I'm not sure what it means.

'I've got something special for you to do today, your first job!'

She's excited about it but I can still taste her anxiety atoms in the air.

'The holiday house needs cleaning, top to bottom. There will be guests coming soon for half-term so I thought this time you could do it. You can try by yourself, now you're older.'

A job. By myself. I should be bouncing with happiness but Mam doesn't usually talk so fast, almost desperate. And what is 'half a term'? I'm older, yes, how old? Have I changed age? There are so many clues that are slipping out that I don't want to interrupt in case there's more so I just smile. Even more important than that – holiday guests are coming, earlier than usual. I could be on the verge of getting my first friend and I'll get to see inside the house they'll stay at. I've never been in anyone else's house, not even the cottages at the bottom of the village.

For the tiniest moment, an image flashes into my mind. I'm at the door of the holiday house and Mam pushes me in with a witch's broom and locks the door, trapping me forever. So ridiculous. I must let the happiness in. I don't know why it's bouncing off me today.

'Let's walk over. I've got everything ready for you.' She inspects my face, checking what my reaction is, the same as I'm checking hers. I'm being too quiet. I mustn't set off her alarms otherwise she may change her mind about letting me do the job by myself.

Mam is wearing her lilac dress today with the bottom half that swirls. She has washed her hair and dried it with the hairdryer instead of naturally so that it's more behaved than usual. Her eyes look different. No, it's her eyelashes. They're the wrong colour, darker. They remind me of the cows with their fanned eyelashes around huge eyeballs. She's really trying to make my first day at work special.

I rattle on as we head down the road. 'I'll make it so shiny and clean! Have you got the apple-scented spray? I like it more than the lemon which is a bit toilety. Although I don't mind cleaning the toilet because it's important to do a thorough job.' I want to ask so many questions. Why did the owner choose me to clean it when we've never met? How come you're letting me do this by myself? Is the lilac dress for me or somebody else? I daren't ask those so stick with something safer.

'Is this my job? Will I be going to work from now on? I don't mind. I can learn how to be really good at it.'

I don't add my burning query of whether this means I'll see the inside of lots more houses. I could clean every building in the village. Or could it possibly mean I will go outside of the village for my work? Could that happen if I do a good job today?

Mam holds out her hand to stop me from walking. 'No, Cate! Oh my goodness, no. This is a one-off, or maybe a couple of times a year. You are a child. Children don't have jobs. They don't work. They play and learn and grow into wonderful humans like you from being given the freedom they deserve. Do you understand?'

I'm not sure I do.

She's looking at me so intensely. I can't figure out why it's so important to her that I don't work but it definitely is. She's talking about now and not-now, me and not-me. I think this means Mam had to work when she was a child. Was she a cleaner or maybe had to work on the farm every day, never playing or having time with her own mother, who she hardly mentions? It seems like the more I try to figure Mam out, the less I know her and the further away we are from one another. I need to smooth things over.

'That's good! I like the way things are. Doing a job today then back to normal tomorrow sounds brilliant.'

Mam starts to walk again; the repair is made. I skip the rest of the way to show that I'm happy and I'm still a child. Mam never skips. 'Is it still called a zoologist if you study people?'

'No, that's only for other animals. There are anthropologists. They research humans and how they live. Or there are psychologists who study the human mind and when things go wrong with it.'

Mam's lips tighten into a smaller mouth that I don't like. I'm making mistakes today with questions. Whatever I think is neutral seems to send Mam back into her head to things she doesn't want to think about. There's no way I can ask her more about what a psychologist does or how our minds go wrong, but I transfer it to my question list because I can tell it hit one of Mam's sore spots.

As we arrive at the holiday house, I feel the enormity of

what's about to happen, like I'm stepping into a new chapter of my story. Mam unlocks the door and shows me all the equipment and cleaning products laid out in the hallway. I pretend to focus as she talks me through what each is for but really I'm trying to absorb every little detail of the house and compare it to ours. Straight ahead is a room with a sofa and huge screen on the wall although I can't see the computer tower so I'm not sure it works. There are glass doors with white plastic edging that look out onto a small garden. The floor isn't shiny and wipeable like ours. The stairs have the same salmon-pink material on them as the hallway.

We walk down the hall to the kitchen. Instead of an island with stools, all the appliances and cooking areas are along the edge of the room, leaving a big space that you could run or dance in.

Down the bottom of the room is a dining table with six chairs. Imagine six people living in a house all at once! How will they all fit upstairs to go to sleep?

'It's mostly dust as there's been nobody here for so long. You have to dust the surfaces first before you do the floors. Brush in here, vacuum for all the other rooms that are carpeted.' Mam looks at me expectantly. I don't have to fake my joy. The strange thing is that despite my nerves earlier of being left alone here, now I can't wait for her to go so I can check out the whole place by myself.

'I'll be fine now. It will be fun! Am I allowed to open the windows for some air?'

Mam runs her fingers along the kitchen windowsill, in between jars filled with different types of pasta and pots of cooking implements, until she finds a small silver key.

'Of course, good idea! This opens all of the windows, make sure you return it to here when you're done so we don't lose it.' She knew where it was. I wonder if Mam usually does the cleaning and has now handed the job over to me. I'm not going to ask any more questions, not on such a perfect day.

I run up the stairs. There are four doors. To the right is a bathroom with a small bath, toilet and instead of a shower cubicle the showerhead hangs over the bath.

The next room along has two beds the same size as mine with a bedside table between them. There are curtains not blinds which are covered in faded roses. From here, I can see Hart Hill and the woods. The windowsill paint is chipped in places. Cobwebs dangle from the corners of the bedroom ceiling – I'll have to deal with those before I clean.

A mirrored wardrobe runs the length of the room. I step onto one of the beds so I can see myself from head to toe. I wonder if I look like Mam did when she was a girl? I know she has photos from then but she says they're in storage, which I think means locked into boxes. I lie on the bed nearest to the window. The ceiling has a bumpy white pattern all over it which is in the shape of a flower around the light. Instead of bulbs set into the ceiling, all the lights here dangle down with cylinder covers over them. I think this is what old houses looked like.

The next room has the most amazing bed which makes me giggle and I kind of wish Mam was here to laugh with me. It is one bed on top of another! The mattresses are bare. There are folded sheets at the bottom of each bed for me to put on. I have to climb onto the top bed to do it. Once I climb up, the ceiling feels too close to my head so I lie flat to see what it must feel like for the people who stay here and sleep away from their homes.

I asked Mam once about why people come here in the summer. 'Haven't they got their own house to be in?'

Mam was using a fast jet of water to zap the dirt from the flagstones in the backyard, making them change from antique to new. 'Yes they have, but they come here to have a change.

Mostly to have some peace and quiet and enjoy the scenery. You're a lucky girl because you get to be in Halham all year round instead of just a couple of weeks.'

Then she'd turned the jet onto my bare feet and legs, chasing me around with water as I screeched and giggled, letting the water catch me so I could feel the cold blast against my skin.

'They come to Halham, but they're strangers. How do we know they're safe to be here?'

Mam turned the hose back to the stones, aiming at weeds that had grown between the cracks. 'Don't worry, I know they're carefully selected people. Usually those who need some quiet to work in. They're here for peace, Cate, so we leave them alone and they leave us alone.' Sometimes Mam gives me rules without them sounding like rules. I have to pay close attention to what is chat and what is instruction.

I don't know who selected the people for the holiday house but it did seem to be mostly quiet people. There had been an old man who carried a black, rectangular bag everywhere with him as he walked his dog.

Once there had been a couple with a baby but it was small and floppy so couldn't play or talk.

The year before, there were two men and two women who were always driving in and out of the village. I sometimes heard music and laughter from the cottage even without going close to it. I'd panicked at the smell of smoke one evening but Mam wasn't worried. She said they were cooking their food outside for fun.

I'd heard the engine of their car so dashed out to the backyard to play hopscotch near the road. A lady with short, blonde hair and wearing black glasses waved to me from the backseat. She looked a bit younger than Mam. By the time I thought to wave back she'd already gone. After that, Mam called me in for school work then we went to the field to do jobs and I never saw the lady again.

I'm not sure I like being on the high bed with the ceiling so close to my face like I'm trapped in a coffin so I put the covers on as quickly as possible then jump down. The wardrobe and drawers are wooden like mine but have been painted a light grey colour, the grain showing faintly through the paint.

From here, I can see the outside cooker in the garden and a wooden table with chairs where the holiday people can sit and talk together. I get a soft cloth and wipe the window ledge where dark spots of mould have started to grow. The apple-scented spray makes the windowpane fuzzy so the shapes in the garden becomes blobs of colour.

I imagine Mam standing by the outdoors cooker making her stuffed peppers. Brown sits opposite his friend, their knees touching out of sight under the table.

The smiling holiday lady from the back of the car has brought her music player and dances on the grass. A man stands looking out to Hart Hill so I can't see his face. He is somebody's father.

Mam calls up to this bedroom window, inviting me down to join them. Or maybe she's shouting to tell me to stay upstairs, that the party is only for grown-ups?

I keep rubbing the glass until it clears and shows the empty garden below.

The last bedroom is the biggest. It has windows both at the front and back of the house making it long and light. The bed in here is huge. Every time I get one corner of the fitted sheet to stay, it pings off when I try to pull the other side down. It's too tricky by myself. The mattress is warm and leaves a dent where my knees stick into it. When I move, the material slowly pulls back into shape. It's what Mam has – memory foam. I place both hands on the bare mattress to soak up any memories of whoever slept here last but I can't make them out. Maybe it's been too long since they left them.

I used to climb into Mam's bed if I woke in the night. It was big enough to have one side each. I wasn't allowed on her side so I never had a chance to soak up her memories. But I always slept really well in her bed, with my knees curled up and sucking my thumb.

I can't remember the last time I went into Mam's room. One day she said I was a big girl and needed to get back to sleep by myself, then turned around so I couldn't see her face. Her shoulders had jiggled a little bit so I thought she might be laughing at a funny joke. I waited and waited but she didn't say, *that was a joke, come in,* so I went back to my own room and shut the door.

It takes ages to sort all the beds, dust the surfaces and vacuum the carpets with a funny cleaner that has a face. My hands and knees ache but I'm so pleased with how lovely it all looks, ready for new guests. I enjoyed it but I also have that peculiar feeling back in my stomach. The bed that was too soft, the bed that was too high and the beds that were too far apart – it reminds me of Goldilocks. *Who's been sleeping in my bed?* Any moment, the bears may come back and find me; a girl who doesn't belong.

I take a rest to eat the sandwiches that Mam packed in a cool-box for me. She's cut up some fruit in lidded bowls like she used to when I was little. I take my food through into the back garden and eat at the wooden table. It doesn't seem like I'm still in Halham. From down here with trees all around the edges of the garden, Hart Hill is out of sight. I could be anywhere, nestled in my chocolate house in the woods.

I take a walk around the small rectangular garden. At the back is a blue shed with one window missing. The door is half-covered by a tree with white flowers. I push the branches back.

There's a lock on the door but it hasn't been pressed together. It looks old and rusty. Inside, there's a patterned rug with faded colours, a bench, a bag with skittles in, and a bike that's twisted at funny angles. A metal rack in the corner is crammed with paint pots, garden tools and pots. Items from a busy family life of fun, games and gardening together.

I leave the shed and pull the stiff door closed. Out behind it, plants are overgrown. Now I'm up close I can see the fencing here isn't straight. There are spiky nettles and weeds that I've never seen before, all fighting one another for space.

One of the fence panels has partly come away and juts out at a strange angle. There's just enough space for a dog to squeeze through – which wouldn't be safe at all: it could escape and get lost. I crouch down to peek through the gap. It leads out to a path in the woods behind Halham that leads all the way to Hart Hill. It's not a place for girls. It could be dangerous. Perhaps there's space for a person to get through, if they made their body as small as possible? I reach out and wiggle my fingers on the other side of the broken fence.

My hand is out of Halham. My hand is in Hart Hill woods.

I snatch it back and rub it with the hand that has never left. My hands don't match anymore. My heart feels funny, like it's taking more beats than it needs to. It seems like there aren't enough oxygen particles in the air so I have to sniff really hard to get some.

I need to get back to the cottage and finish my job. That's the important thing. Mam has trusted me so I mustn't let her down. As I head back, I flash a glance back towards the shed, satisfied that there's nothing obvious to show that just for a moment, a part of me left the village.

Back in the kitchen, I take careful stock of each item of furniture. I list them from left to right in my head to soothe away the agitation. Cupboard, cupboard, drawer, sink. Cabinet, table, six chairs. It's a mix of all different kinds of wood and shapes. The dresser is a darker wood than the main kitchen furniture. It has lots of little drawers. I pull out a couple. They are stiff and need a good yank which sends vibrations up my arms. One drawer has mismatched cutlery. Another has rectangular boards.

I keep looking through, turning the items over to see the differences from our things. The plates and bowls are not plain but blue and white patterned around the edges. The centre is a scene with a little house, trees, a boat on water and two birds. A whole world on a plate! Why would you want to cover it with food?

There are glasses of all different shapes and sizes. My favourite are four thin, tall glasses with stems that are decorated with gold squiggly lines. Most of the drawers are empty so I guess the holidaymakers can put their own belongings inside that they bring from home so they don't feel too far away and lonely.

It's only at the very end of looking through that I realise that above all the little drawers is one long, flat drawer that is sneaky because it just looks like a piece of wood and has no handle. I pull it out. There is red velvet lining which is marked in some places. I find a couple of old keys, some nails and a folded piece of paper. I flatten out the paper at the dining table.

It's a receipt like the ones Mam has from our accounts of the farm that she keeps in a locked filing cabinet. It's not yellow and it wasn't cleared out when the cottage was cleaned so maybe it's recent. It shows the cost of renting the holiday house to Mr Andrew Baddeley. Perhaps that was the man with the briefcase and dog, two summers ago? I read and reread the next line.

Paid in full to Ms Imogen Laverly.

That's Mam's surname, Laverly? So that's my surname too. *Catelyn Laverly.* I never thought to ask. Imogen and Cate seemed enough. Saying my whole name makes me sound more real, part of a world where there's so much more than Mam and me.

The receipt also tells me something else important. The holiday house belongs to us. It's been ours this whole time.

12

IMOGEN

NOW

Imogen had no intention of letting Zach in after she first read his letter. There were too many risks involved. She allowed herself to travel to their past in her daydreams but never an imagined present. And there could be no future.

But over the last few days, she found herself caught up in her childhood game of imagining horrific outcomes. It was different now; all the tragedies happened to her rather than others, leaving Cate all alone. The barn could catch fire while she tended to it, trapping her in a smoke-filled space with nobody around to rescue her. Inside, hay would ignite easily, spreading to the wooden structure which would fall to pieces around her as she choked on fumes.

Or one of Grove's horses could take fright and kick her in the temple, causing a brain injury so that she no longer knew who she was, never mind Cate, and was unable to provide the basics of food and care.

Perhaps her arteries were already hardened, a small clot building up to cut off her blood supply one morning so that her daughter would find her face-down in the field surrounded by flies.

On and on her mind went, churning out disasters.

Imogen had done so much – everything – to protect her girl. But if she weren't around, Cate would be completely vulnerable and unable to forge a life for herself here. Imogen's deliberate pruning of all non-essential contacts meant there was no back-up plan.

Is that what Zach could become? Imogen doesn't agree with the self-obsessed statement that "everything happens for a reason". His letter is more likely to be a test than a solution. And yet. Zach knows her history and at one point had loved her. He may be her only chance. The risk is that if she tells him the truth about Cate, Father, herself, he may try to destroy the thing she wishes him to protect: Cate's life at Halham.

Imogen glugs a glass of iced water. Sweat gathers at her hairline, certain to make the hairs there curl into disobedience. She pulls the material of her dress away from her clammy skin and tries to slow down her breathing.

The house looks too pristine, as if she's made an effort for Zach's visit. Imogen throws an old blanket over the sofa and knocks down a pile of books that were stacked by the bookcase. Perhaps she should change out of her dress into her dungarees and walking boots? She doesn't know when Zach will arrive and the uncertainty frustrates her desire for careful planning. He gave no time in his letter.

It was ridiculous to be ready so early with Cate out of the way; perhaps he wouldn't arrive until late afternoon. There's a chance that Cate will finish her cleaning or need some help and so she may come home to find Zach in the house. Imogen's head feels tight and throbbing, too many possibilities fan out, all of which end in catastrophe.

She grabs a bag, fills it with items from Cate's room and the kitchen, then marches up to the holiday house.

Inside the hall, the chemically-derived scent of apples

makes her gag. She mustn't let her worry show through her mask. Cate has always been good at picking up on any waves in her well-being, even as a toddler. She'd cover her stress with speed.

'Cate, it's me, I've got to pop off but I've got some of your things here.'

Cate runs into the hallway with flushed cheeks from exertion. She's glowing with anticipation. 'Come and see everything!'

Imogen isn't sure how this dynamic developed. Cate has always loved to show her what she's done, as if to please her mattered more than doing it. Imogen rushes around the house doling out praise and, to be fair, Cate has done an excellent job. She can't help but see a snapshot of what could have been, in different circumstances, the two of them running a rental business and taking time to be great hosts to visitors.

'I've got some jobs to do at the house but I've had an idea. You know you've always wanted to go camping in the field?' She can't bear to look at Cate now, guessing that her face has lit up. 'Well, I thought it might be fun for you to sleep here, as if you're on holiday. You could open the French doors onto the garden because it's safe here, the garden is fenced off. That would kind of be like camping because this sofa turns into a bed.'

Cate freezes. Her eyes grow wide. In that moment, she turns from teen girl to a painting of a cherub: delicate and unsure, belonging to a different world. 'You mean on my *own?*'

Imogen makes herself busy moving Cate's belongings out of the hall into the living room and pulls open the sofa bed, throwing the cushions to the side. She needs to get back home. Zach could be at the gates right now. There's a chance he may drive past if she's not waiting for him.

'Yes! Well, I mean, I'll come up later and bring some dinner. We can eat together and see how you get on?'

A compromise. It would be so much easier if she could throw her arms around Cate for comfort.

Imogen makes the sofa bed up and finds herself taking far too long trying to stroke away each crease in the duvet cover. It's an awkward size, halfway between single and double so the fit isn't good. Two people would have to snuggle close to share it. Imogen plumps up both pillows and lays them on top of the duvet, all the while avoiding eye contact with her daughter.

Cate hovers in the corner of the room. Uncertainty emanates from her. The buzz of childlike energy has converted into agitation. Imogen thinks of a hapless fly repeatedly bashing against a closed window.

'Here, if you pull back the voiles there's such a lovely view of the garden, you can see it even when you lie down. We can call it our own version of camping.'

As usual, the norms are adapted for their life. So many not-quite-rights. There's no time to dwell. Imogen pulls out a bag of mints and empties them into a glass bowl, waves her goodbye and leaves before Cate can start a round of questioning.

As Imogen flees down the path to the gates, she can't help but feel the tug of guilt of a mother who has left her incredulous three-year-old at nursery for the first time. It feels like a betrayal. But Cate is thirteen years old, almost as tall as her and on the cusp of biological womanhood. Has she done the wrong thing in trying to give her a protected childhood? No, no. It's the outside world that does it wrong. Imogen can't take the blame for a skewed society. Everything she has done for Cate was for her own good and one day she'll understand and thank her.

It doesn't seem right to Imogen to wait in the house. Perhaps she shouldn't let Zach inside at all to taint its newness with their history. She walks along the access road to Halham, down to Beggars Lane. Fields of green and yellow fan back to distant hills. Traffic is sparse along this route.

From the grass verge, Imogen can see the spire of St Michael's church peeping over hedgerows. Her parents had never been Christians but people presumed Father was a religious man. He'd had a way of speaking in public that was calm and assured. His voice seemed to hold more attention the quieter it became, as if only those who paid close attention would understand and benefit from his messages. He was a preacher in his own way. The villagers had needed someone and something to believe in when the god of their childhoods left prayers unanswered. Father knew how to say just enough to allow the listeners to add their own interpretations to his statements, moulded to fit whatever hole gaped inside them. She could almost hear his voice again, preaching to the villagers.

'Faith is not blind. It is the opposite; it is approached with eyes open in wonder! Look at the world as if it's new to you. It can become new to you, here and now.' He had paused between each statement but retained command with his head tilted upwards. Nobody ever interrupted him, no matter their desperation. 'Your body is part of nature. As much as the wheat you grow, the cattle you tend, the blackbirds that sing out around us. Nature is cyclical. It regenerates and replenishes each year, as you all know.'

Imogen had always loved to listen to Father's speeches. Even when things became strained between them as she railed against the Rounds, his voice continued to mesmerise her. In her head she could think poetically but that never translated to her speech. Imogen felt awkward and insufficient around Father's eloquence. She learnt to use the power of silence. This seemed to suit them both. Opposite strengths had made them a successful duo.

Now she's trying to sing two parts of parenting for her daughter but it's not the same. She has her own void that can't be filled. Grief never leaves. Complicated grief is where the pain of loss is as strong as the pain that was caused by the same person. It tries to pull her down, like clothes on a drowning man.

The church bells ring in the new hour to demand that Imogen returns from her reverie. What does the outside world care about her? There's relief to no longer be a special girl. But the only viable alternative was to become invisible. She's so weary of it all. The effort. The forward planning. The thought that must go into every single daily task in order to live a life that protects her daughter's right to a carefree childhood. It's worth it of course – to see Cate skip with the abandonment of a child with no guilt or responsibility, who knows only unconditional love. And yet, here she is, a mother standing on the roadside, waiting to meet the man who once meant more to her than anything else.

Imogen sees the blue camper-van from a good distance as the lane is long and straight running parallel to Halham. What had she expected? Not this. It seems almost comical that Zach arrives this way. If they were teenagers again, he could throw open the door for her to jump in next to him, driving off together without ever turning back. But she's nearly thirty-one and a mother. Imogen waves the vehicle into the access road to be out of sight and runs behind.

'Hey, you.' It's Zach. He climbs out of the van as gracefully as a cat and stretches his arms upwards. There are a few grey strands on his temple, a softening of the jawline, but it's him. He's dressed in a white V-neck T-shirt and blue jeans, timeless. His hair blows in the breeze as his head is cocked slightly to the side. She mustn't stare. The two of them are back at Halham together for the first time in thirteen and half years.

Zach hadn't known that Cate was growing inside Imogen

back then. If he had, everything would have turned out differently. She could have told the truth about Father and her pregnancy to keep the man she loved. But in the end, she'd loved her baby more than him and she hadn't wanted to share it.

13

CATE

It's special to be somewhere new but the weird thing is that I can't help wishing I was back in my own house. From the sofa, I can see out into the garden. The contented trees sway against a blue sky. It's perfect but it's different. Everything smells of strangers so I fling open the doors to let in the familiar scents from outside.

My body isn't happy. It's jittery like there's too much electricity inside so I can't keep still. Cells in the brain are called neurons. They look like starfish that have been made out of rubber with each tentacle stretched out too far. The neurons talk to each other using electricity so no wonder my mind won't shut up right now with so much zapping around inside me.

To calm the electricity waves, I become a scientist. That means thinking about one problem at a time and trying to find the evidence to solve it. I'm going to try to work out more about Mam's mind and behaviour – like a psychologist.

Mam knows things from a long time ago: old, antique and even ancient things. Other times she knows impossible things. Dinosaurs existed a long time before humans. Mam taught me about different types and we looked at pictures of their fossils which is their bones turned into rock. In our lesson, I was wondering what it would have been like to be near a real, live dinosaur. Mam looked away like she does when she's looking at things inside her head.

'See your cup of water, there? Imagine it would ripple from the centre with each boom-boom footstep of the *T. rex*. That's how you'd know he was approaching.'

It hasn't ever happened, a human with their cup of water near a stomping dinosaur, but Mam said it as sure as if she'd seen it with her own eyes. That's when I started to wonder what happens when she goes away in her head. Where does she really go?

Mam also gets that faraway look when I haven't asked a question at all. She used to do that a lot more when I was younger, sometimes for days on end. Sometimes her face is blank, zero out of ten, but other times it's like she's watching her memories playing out in the room right in front of us; ghosts that only she can see. That's when things have gone very wrong and Mam doesn't want to be in this world with me. She travels, I think. To another place or another time. It might be when things get to eleven out of ten so that keeping busy doesn't work anymore. That's what happened with the baby bird incident.

The chick must have dropped from its nest before it was ready to fly. It had fallen onto moss by the village walls. It was curled over and floppy, not moving at all. It was kind of horrible to look at without its feathers but I felt so sorry for it. I tried to see if its mother was in the nest but I couldn't see anything with all the leaves in the way. I wasn't sure what type of bird it was or how to call out to its family.

I shouted over to Mam who was hanging out our washing on the twirly clothes dryer in the garden. She couldn't hear me, so I cupped the little thing in my hand, keeping its bed of moss underneath its small body. I didn't want to drop or shock it so walked fast but steady with my arms out in front of me. It looked so fragile and naked. It couldn't survive without help.

Mam hummed to herself while pegging out sheets. I thought she'd be happy that I'd taken care of the baby. We're always kind to animals, even the spiders that make my skin feel prickly with their fast, scuttering movements.

'Look, the baby bird needs help. I don't know if it's still alive.' I held my hand out to Mam. I wasn't sure if she could see properly but she dropped the sheet in shock as if I'd done something cruel to that chick. She came running over, grabbed my sleeve and pulled me over to the hedge, trying to yank my arm up.

'Get rid of it, throw it now, you mustn't touch it.' I didn't have time to explain about the moss or say I hadn't touched his bird-skin. I knew I wasn't allowed to touch the fluffy farm cat but I wasn't sure about the rules for a baby bird and just wanted to do the right thing. I didn't want to throw it, that didn't seem right. I pulled my arm away and backed off from Mam, tears clouding my view of her. It didn't make sense.

Mam's voice hardened. 'Put that chick down this instant and get to your room.' I could feel the heat of her anger burn into me. Her mouth was a straight line cutting across her face. I laid the bird down as gently as I could then ran into the house without looking back to see what happened next.

In the bathroom, I locked the door and sat on the toilet, crying and shaking. What had I done wrong that she was so very cross with me? Then I washed my hands with warm water and lavender soap. They still felt wrong, so I washed and washed but I couldn't get the yuckiness off me. I sat with my back to the locked door and shrank myself down to spider-size, to ant-size, to a dust-mite, even smaller to an electron: a negative charge too tiny to be seen. Then I waited.

By the time I grew back to girl-size and got into bed, it was dark outside. There was a sandwich placed on my bedside table with a glass of water. I felt stiff and achy. I wanted to see Mam so much but not while she was still upset with me. I couldn't eat any food. Nothing would feel right until Mam and me were back to BFF.

I wondered about the baby bird. Through my bedroom window, the garden was too dark to see clearly. Mam wasn't out there. I didn't know if she was downstairs or had gone out into Halham, leaving me all alone. Or if she'd gone even further away.

I crept along the hallway, needing to know if Mam was in the house. Without her, it seemed like the glass might fall right out of the windows, each metal support dropping down one by one, until all the walls fell, leaving me standing alone in a pile of broken pieces. I listened outside Mam's door but couldn't hear her breathing or turning the pages in a book, sighing about a long day with her feet propped up on the foot rest.

Downstairs, the lights were off in the kitchen and dining room. The final place she could be in the house was her study. As the door was half-open, I peeked through the gap with one eye. Mam was on her reading chair, staring straight ahead of her. Two tears slid down her cheek and dropped onto her rose blouse. That made my heart ache the most. I wasn't sure if Mam was really in our world or if she'd left her body here while she travelled in her mind, up out of now, to a past or future where I didn't exist. I had seen Mam like this before and knew it could take a long time to get her back.

I wanted to change what had happened that day but it was too late. I couldn't make the chick's mother swoop down to pick its baby up with its beak, flying it back to the nest to recover. I couldn't change the expression on Mam's face as I crossed the garden with the bird in my hand or the way she snapped at me. The scene was set and couldn't be altered. Instead, question after question filled my head, enough to fill a whole notebook if I'd had the energy to write them down. Why had the chick fallen like that close to the house? Why was I the one who found it? Why was it so very terrible that I had picked it up?

That's the first time I had the new idea about why there was too much danger for me to get close to people or leave the village. Perhaps it wasn't about keeping me safe from men, war, history, or strangers.

I realised the most awful thing and now I'm in the holiday house all alone, I can't stop thinking about it.

Maybe the reason I can't be touched or ever leave the village is because I'm the one who's dangerous.

14
___

IMOGEN

NOW

The camper-van seemed too intimate for their reunion so Imogen invited Zach to the house. She strode ahead to avoid being close to him. Now they stand awkwardly in the kitchen as almost-strangers.

'It's good to see you.' Zach flashes a shy smile then makes a show of looking around the room. 'It's such a different type of house. Nice, though, how you've done it.'

Imogen flinches at the forced lightness of his tone. Neither of them alludes to what happened the last time they were together at Halham.

'I had it built with Father's money. Something light and new for...' She almost said *us*. For the past thirteen years, everything had been about Cate and her together, as if she didn't exist in her own right.

'Inheritance, yes.' That word says everything that they're not acknowledging to one another. Zach moves to stand at the back window facing the garden. 'You always wanted a vegetable patch, I remember that. You thought you'd be self-sufficient that way.'

Perhaps it was inevitable that she'd end up so cut off from the world; she willed it into coming true.

'It's mirrored glass; we can see out but nobody can see in.' Imogen doesn't know why she just said that. She digs her nails into her arm to try to regain control. *Why the hell did she invite him into their home?*

Zach turns towards her. She tries not to breathe too deeply so she doesn't catch his scent. The stubble on his neck looks as if it would be rough to the touch. Imogen feels the cracks in her composure. Even eye contact feels too sensuous after such a long time by herself.

'Who'd be there to look inside, anyway?'

Damn.

A decision needed to be made about the parameters of her honesty with him. Imogen couldn't have spoken even if she wanted to. Her mouth was robbed of all its saliva. The back of her throat was constricted with barely enough space to breathe. Imogen forces herself to look over at the fridge to where she'd removed photographs of her and Cate together. She'd wanted time to explain. If only she could tell the whole story, then Zach would maybe understand. But the time for words has passed.

Imogen pulls one of the photographs from the kitchen drawer. Cate is around six years old wearing a pink tutu with a trowel in one hand and a bucket in the other. She always loved this photo of her daughter who was unconstrained by social expectations of what a girl should be; evidence of the benefits of her growing up without the harm of external forces. Cate's grin shows a gap where two of her two lower teeth had come out. Imogen had wrapped the first tooth she lost in tissue paper and told her daughter to put it under the pillow for the tooth fairy. Cate had looked confused as it was the first time she'd ever heard of such a thing.

Zach walks over as slow and steady as if he's approaching an unearthed hand grenade. Imogen places the photograph into the warmth of his palm. Then she grabs two more – a picture where Imogen is still so young and fresh holding her baby in wonder; and a recent photo of twelve-year-old Cate sitting on the tyre swing with her long limbs pointing to Hart Hill.

Zach looks from one to another carefully. Imogen's ribcage tightens.

'I don't understand.' He goes back to the photograph that shows Imogen as he'd recall her. Short hair, young skin, eighteen years old. 'You never told me. Is she here? Is she mine?'

It took the first few years of Cate's life for Imogen to learn how to shut down the tsunami of feelings that overwhelmed her. She'd cry endlessly, spend time in bed or staring into space, or scrub at the tiles until the pain in her wrists and knees became even worse than the pain inside her heart. But little by little, she'd learnt to put those feelings away and wrapped her attention and time so carefully around her little girl that there was no room for anything else.

Until now.

Imogen had pushed away memories of Zach so often and so far that he seemed unreal. She leans her head into Zach's chest and sobs from her stomach upwards. He holds her and doesn't speak another word.

'I'm so sorry, so sorry, Zach.'

But it's not the time for Imogen to explain all the things she is sorry about. She can't risk it yet. There's a kind of grief that rises up to take hold of her. It doesn't belong to this moment. She must clamber on top of it to continue with what needs to be done.

After what seems like an impossibly long time, Zach takes Imogen's hand and leads her to the dining table. They sit opposite each other. He lays out the photographs of Cate in front of him. Thirteen years of life condensed into a row of three pictures.

'You should have told me. I'd have come back in a heartbeat, no matter what the consequences were.'

Under the table, Imogen digs her nails into her thighs. He thinks she didn't know about the baby on the night it all went wrong. His trust in her hurts more than the anger she'd imagined. She is undeserving, that much is clear but she isn't doing this for herself.

Zach is a pale ghost version of the one she recalls. His carefree spirit in youth that liberated her from the chains of Father's expectation has diminished. He runs his index finger along the baby photo. There's no going back. This is one more thing Imogen has stolen from him.

Touch. How will she explain to Zach that it's best if he doesn't hug Cate? Imogen never stopped Zach from touching her, no matter how exhausted she was from the Rounds. It seemed impossible to Imogen that being close to Zach would cause any drain on her. Perhaps it wouldn't harm Cate either? He seems healthy enough. But rules had to be abided by in all circumstances. It would only confuse Cate if the rules around touch weren't clear.

'I survived by living a certain kind of life. With Cate.' How does she condense over a decade of this life for someone who hasn't lived it?

Zach mouths the name *Cate*, trying it out for the first time. Imogen drags her eyes away from his lips. She fetches a jug of water with tumblers to escape the intensity of the moment. Two matching glasses. Everything she bought new is in pairs. There was never meant to be anybody else here.

'So, how come you let me visit this time? I wrote to you for over a year after I left. Our phone calls back and forth where you seemed to be talking to someone you barely knew. I thought you froze me out because of your father; that was why you couldn't bear to see me.'

'It was the best way I could see to make things manageable. And it gave you the chance at a new life with none of our history dragging you down.'

Zach runs his fingers through his hair; that old sign of uncertainty. Imogen sips the icy water to pull herself back from the image of Zach at seventeen. The sweetness of his uncertainty in those days. A different kind of hunger they'd had for each other's bodies that had nothing to do with sickness and desperation.

'It wouldn't have been a drag. We could have supported each other. I loved you so much. I only stopped trying because you had good reason to hate me by then.'

Imogen had never hated Zach. She had learnt a trick to gather all her love for him and Father and pour it into her daughter. Why has she let him back in to her life and Halham despite the risks? Years of careful planning have come to nothing now Imogen is faced with the past.

'Your letter took me by surprise. I wasn't sure what to do about your visit. I wanted to do what was best for Cate. That's how I've made all my decisions.'

Zach sips his water. 'I guess she's getting to an age where she might want to have a say in decisions that affect her? I would have liked the chance to choose back then.' He speaks carefully, his frustration only leaking out in the flush of his cheeks. Imogen had only ever seen him lose control once.

'Can we talk another time? I have to go and check on Cate and take her some food. It's too soon for you to meet. She's sensitive. I'll have to prepare her.'

Zach looks around. Worry creases his brow. 'Where is she?'

'She's up at the old house, having a sleepover.' Villagers had described her old home as a "chocolate-box cottage". They saw the perfect home and none of what went on indoors. Once she needed an income, Imogen renamed it as the holiday house. That's all Cate had ever known it as. Each piece of information Imogen reveals to Zach feels dangerous. Her head throbs. She needs him to leave the house.

'Is she with friends?'

Imogen shakes her head. This was going to be difficult to explain. Cate has no friends. She has her mother. What if Zach doesn't understand or agree with the life she's chosen as best for her daughter? For *their* daughter?

It's too late now. The house of cards is collapsing. Imogen's acceptance of Zach's request to visit has set something in motion that she can no longer prevent.

He says, 'Look, I could stay in the van tonight and we can talk properly tomorrow while Cate's at school?'

Imogen's stomach churns. She knows her breathing is too fast but she can't master it. Her fingers start to tingle. She grabs her bag and the tray of food she'd already prepared. 'Could you come back at the weekend? Bring some things. I need a few days.'

Imogen realises that she never asked where Zach had been heading up north. He could have a wife and young children waiting there for him. She was so used to blotting out the outside world that it felt almost irrelevant.

Zach follows her out of the door. They squint in the evening light to the far end of the estate. 'It all looks the same from here, like I've never been away.'

'Well, you have been away for a very long time.' Imogen pulls the front door shut behind her, taking extra care that the lock clicks into place. 'It's all different. I'm different.'

She turns and walks away towards the old cottages, unsure if what she just said is true.

15

———

CATE

Our house smells wrong. I came back as soon as the sky lightened this morning. I barely slept on the sofa bed. I've never been away from home overnight. Even though I told my brain, *It's still Halham. It's still the safest village in England,* my body didn't believe it. The metal poles beneath me had squeaked at the slightest movement. My eyes kept opening without me telling them to.

It was a relief when the edges of the curtains started to glow and the birds sang their morning welcome. I locked the holiday house then placed my hand against its rough stone walls as a way for it to remember me. Then I slung my bag on my back and took the quickest route home instead of stopping at the playground on the way. I missed our house almost as much as I'd missed Mam.

Everything looks the same in the kitchen but it doesn't feel right. There are the correct number of pans inside one another in the corner. The spices in the rack all face forwards. I pull down the dishwasher door but it's empty already – Mam must have washed her dishes by hand last night instead. There's a change in the air that I can't describe. It's not like perfume or sweat but an in-between scent. If it was a metal, it would be ancient, heavy gold with flecks of black. I feel like I've walked into a copy of my own house instead of the real thing where the person who made it got all the parts right but the soul of it wrong.

A stranger has been here. Another person has been right inside our house and stayed long enough that they've left tiny particles of themselves behind. I think of the farm dogs sniffing in the morning to find where the foxes have been in the night. Outsiders leave a trail, even if they don't mean to. I try to look for clues in the dining room, the study and the living room but I don't really know what they would be. The other rooms seem the same as always. The back door is locked and so are all the windows.

It's not an intruder if someone lets them in.

Mam must be at home and still asleep because it's so early. There's no way that she wouldn't be. My sleepover in the holiday house was an exciting treat after doing well with cleaning, that's all. I creep upstairs and put my ear to the narrow gap where Mam hasn't fully shut her door. I hear her exhale and let my own breath out. I knew she'd be there.

I do a quick check upstairs but nothing feels wrong here, only back in the kitchen. I flop onto my bed. My pillow squishes down just the right amount unlike the puffy pillow in the holiday house. I'd missed it. I'd missed the stripes of light that shine through my blinds instead of flowery curtains, and the thwack of my feet on our tiles instead of silent carpet, and the background sounds that tell me Mam is busy around the house only a few metres from me instead of being all alone.

What if Mam didn't miss me because she has a secret?

I draw my knees up to my stomach and wait. I need to do something to stop the crawling sensation at the back of my neck. The best thing to do is to put things back into order.

In my mind, I go through the rooms I'd been in at the holiday house. The room with two beds is: beds, bedside cabinet, lamp, wardrobe. The bathroom is: basin, bath, mat, shower, toilet. As I say each word, I can imagine what each item feels like under my fingertips, even if I never touched it in real life. I can feel the red velvet of the secret drawer, soft and squishy apart from where it was worn away. The folded receipt is crisp and dry. The shed lock is cold and rough in places where the rust has gathered.

The water pipes vibrate right behind my headboard. That means Mam has flushed the toilet. She's awake at last. I must swallow down my questions and anxiety. She'll explain it all, put everything back the way it should be.

Then we can go out for a walk and see how the lambs are doing. I'll tell her that I slept brilliantly and she'll explain the scent. We can collect the best leaves and petals to make a perfume and put it in one of her glass bottles. We'll call it Halham Hearts and I'll draw a design on the label that means we love each other forever and have our own special scent as a code.

Mam's door opens and I step out to catch her on the landing. It's easier to smile now that I've designed the rest of our morning. In just a few minutes everything will be clear and ready to go.

'I think somebody's been in the house. It smells different. Not cleaning-different but person-different.'

Mam pulls her dressing gown tight across her and knots the cord that usually hangs loose. Her eyelashes are back to their normal colour.

'Good morning to you, too. That sniffer dog nose of yours has been at it again. It was the delivery worker. A different one from usual. By the way, I think you might need these.'

Mam hands me a cardboard box and pulls out one long,

white item. 'It's for bleeding. You pull this sticker off and put it in your pants. There's a special bin for them in the bathroom.'

I can't hide anything from Mam. She hadn't seemed angry about the bleeding. In fact, she had softened her voice like when she used to put me to bed. I called it her cotton-wool voice. I haven't heard it for a while. I hadn't realised I missed it until now. There are special bins just for these blood-pads. So other people must get the bleeding, too. Mam's en-suite has a small silver bin with foot pedal. Does she bleed too? There are so many questions. I will have to lock them in a cupboard in my head for now.

I follow her down the staircase but don't feel like eating. Mam had changed the subject from my question about the scent of another person. What kind of delivery would need to come all the way into the house? How long did he stay to leave his smell behind? I can't explain how I know it's a *he* but there's something about the smell that tells me.

Mam gets her coffee ready but she shuts the cupboard door a little bit harder than usual and tap, tap, taps the spoon on the side of her mug. As she puts the milk back, the fridge door swings past me and I notice what should have been obvious when I was looking for clues. The photos of me that usually hang on there with ladybird magnets have all gone.

'I'll eat later,' I say. 'I think it's too early for me. I'll have some juice.'

We're good at sliding past one another without touching. I get as close as I can to her while I reach for the carton. Mam's shoulder is near my nose. I do a long, deep sniff.

Mam smells of the stranger.

It's a quiet smell but I'm good at paying attention with my nose – I've practised hard out in the fields to become a botanist. I think the scent is in her hair or on her neck. He touched her there. He must have held his hand there for quite some time. Or she leant on him while he stroked her. I push away images of Brown and his friend. This isn't the same. It can't be.

'Well, make sure you eat before too long. You need your energy. I'm going to do some errands.' Mam has barely looked at me. She's kept her eyes busy doing other things. It's as though she doesn't want to be in the same place as me. Instead of travelling in her mind, she's doing it in real life. She always says that men are trouble and that we don't need them.

If Mam was a colour today, she'd be see-through.

I remember when I was younger and had to stand on the stool to reach the front door latch and let myself out. Mam had days of being see-through. It hadn't been her fault. I'd leave the door open and make a track to help her find me when she got her colours back. I had a skipping rope with wooden handles that were chewed on the ends. I snaked it from the door mat to the front of the house. Then, a line of my toys up to where I was playing: bowling pins, cars, dolls, teddy. I left the trail like Hansel and Gretel so Mam wouldn't think she'd lost me when she climbed back into her body.

The front door clicks shut. I watch her as she hurries out of sight towards the far end of the village. She didn't take any food or milk with her for the neighbours. I don't know what kind of errand that could be.

I run up to bed and curl myself under the covers where everything still smells the way it should.

First, Mam got rid of me from the house. Then, she got rid of all evidence that I exist. She would have had good reasons for that. The millipedes turn onto their backs and press their legs against the back of my neck then they run down my arms. The only way to prevent them from biting is to chant the truth in my head over and over. *She had good reasons, we are BFF, this is the safest village in England, we only need each other.*

16
____

IMOGEN

NOW

Ever since Zach visited, Imogen had felt her protective layers start to fray at the edges. She hadn't noticed how muffled and distant she'd made the outside world even when walking in it. Her body did tasks that her mind wasn't fully present for. Now she stands in the post office queue, she feels as if the dial has been turned up on all her senses.

The light above the left-hand desk has a flicker which subtly changes the shadows across the face of the woman who serves her. Her badge says she's called Melody and is happy to help. As she steps down from her stool to fetch Imogen's parcel, Melody sighs with effort. Her ankles are swollen above open-toed sandals. Her second toe reaches out further than the first.

'Here we are, Halham House isn't it?' Melody hands over the parcel. It's a gift for Cate that Imogen has spent hours researching: a chance for them to see the world. There's a scent of the post-mistress's deodorant and last night's menopausal sweat. Melody's middle-aged memory may be pricked by Halham's address. Imogen pulls the material of her linen blouse away from her chest where it scratches as roughly as a hessian sack.

The line of people behind her is a good couple of steps away but she senses the pressure of them pushing forwards. Perhaps they are impatient for their own parcels. Perhaps they'd overheard Melody's announcement of her address and were curious to see what has become of the child healer. Halham – *house of health* in Old English; the place where generations of special little girls had done their duty.

Imogen dips her head down and watches the ground under her feet as she flees into the town. There are so many people. At least half of them hold their phones as they walk. Some talk into them, others stare at screens, glancing up now and then to avoid collisions. It is as much a virtual world as a real one these days and Imogen realises that could suit Cate and her just fine. She holds the parcel in the crook of her left arm like an infant and swerves to walk in the road to avoid pedestrians.

On the opposite side of the road, a cluster of children wriggle around their teacher. They hold hands in pairs, wearing tiny high-vis tabards with 'Oakhurst Nursery' embroidered on the back. The traffic stops to let them cross. Their chatter is high-pitched and frantic with excitement. One girl with thick dark plaits and round cheeks reminds Imogen of a younger Cate. She never stopped talking at that age, relying on the company of pigeons and trees. But she was a happy child. She skipped and laughed and recounted fairy tales with delight, her arms telling the story as much as her mouth. She'd surely gained more than she lost by not attending the rigidity of a village school.

Imogen pulls her gaze away and continues towards the car park, speeding up as she approaches her car. Her hand tremors a little as she scrambles for her keys.

Imogen doesn't turn the engine on. Even the car seems more three-dimensional than usual. The slight bumps in the plastic coating of the steering wheel are warm to the touch. A small insect crawls up the passenger side window, slips down a little, then starts again. The rumble of the main road makes its way up Imogen's legs despite the windows being closed.

'Excuse me!' An elderly man knocks on Imogen's car window. She can't wind the window down with the engine still off so reluctantly cracks open the door. 'Sorry I made you jump, I saw you in the post office and I thought it can't be... But it is, isn't it?'

Imogen recognises the look on his face – desperation. She shouldn't have opened the door.

'I have to go home now.'

The man wraps his fingers around the edges of the car door so Imogen can't pull it shut without trapping his fingers. His knuckles are red and misshapen from arthritis. He seems to be on the verge of tears. That isn't Imogen's problem. She's served her time. Besides, she has nothing of use to give to anyone now and hasn't for over a decade. Imogen leans her head to one side to look past the man, checking that the whole post office queue hasn't followed her.

'It's my daughter, you see.'

Imogen doesn't want to see but it comes to her without intent. A kind, funny forty-one-year-old woman. How it started with pain in her lower back which she dismissed as muscular. The falls that meant she stopped volunteering with asylum seekers at the library. Days in bed that should have been spent holding her youngest – a surprise late baby born with a hole in his heart. The weakness now spreading down her left-hand side. How sometimes it's hard for her to find the right word so she makes jokes, endless jokes, to cover her deficits but in the shower she sobs so hard it hurts.

'It doesn't work anymore. I can't do anything.' *She* can't do anything. And Cate shouldn't have to. Heavy guilt squeezes the air from her lungs. Imogen must protect her own daughter just as this stranger is trying to protect his. 'Remove your hand from my car. You don't have the right. I'm leaving.'

The man's mouth falls open. Imogen mustn't cave. She yanks the door shut as soon as his grasp weakens. As she speeds away, she doesn't look in the rear-view mirror.

Back in the safe familiarity of her study, images from the car park of the old man's daughter with neurological problems are fading. A twinge remains in Imogen's back: an echo of someone else's symptoms or her active imagination? She must focus on what she picked up at the post office.

Imogen removes the plastic viewers from the box. She fiddles with the settings to ensure everything works before calling Cate. The device has several settings that need deactivating; she can't afford any surprises. The programmes are uploaded. Imogen double-checks that she has disconnected from the internet then shouts for Cate to come inside.

'We're going on a mini-break. Come and see!'

Cate arrives breathless. Her face lights up with the wonder of a much younger child. 'You really mean it? Like the trips you did when you were little to the seaside?'

She doesn't know about the Rounds but loves to hear Imogen relay edited details of trips to the seaside or Welsh mountains with Father when she was young.

'It's an extra special way to travel. Very modern. Would you like seaside, mountain or lake?'

Imogen hands over one headset and holds the other up to her own face.

'Is it a teleporter?'

'Not quite but almost as good. You watch through here. The instructions say it's best to sit down at first until you get used to it.'

She shows Cate how to put the headset on then pulls her own down slightly so she can watch her daughter's reaction.

The screens are linked to show the same virtual reality scene. Imogen selects a peaceful lakeside and waterfall, the likes of which she'd never visited in real life. That way it would be new and special for both of them.

Cate gasps at the sight of it. She moves her head slowly from left to right then tips it upwards. The meditation app is 360 degrees of virtual scenery. The gushing sound of the water and the song of distant birds make the scene incredibly realistic.

'Where are we?'

Imogen laughs and pulls her own headset on fully. Swans glide across the lake. Clouds roll by to add a sense of gentle movement of time. Sunlight sparkles on the surface of the lake. She'd forgotten that happens near water, little flashes of light that catch the eye. Cate has never seen a body of water.

'Isn't it fantastic! It's computer-generated. I picked the scene and added elements that I thought we'd like. Do you see the cygnets swimming behind their mother? And a magnolia tree over on the left?'

It had cost a small fortune but would be worth it. The additional money she'd have coming in soon from the holiday house rental would make up for the extra she'd spent this month.

'It's not a real place?'

Imogen pulls the headset up and balances it on the top of her head. She watches Cate stretch her arm out to her left to try to touch the magnolia flowers. The box contains hand-held controllers that can change elements in a scene: make day into night, turn the seasons from this summer paradise to a snowy scene, choose pink blossom over white magnolias. But she didn't want to overwhelm her daughter. Keep things simple. This is a perfect place for them to sit together.

'It is if you believe it to be.' Imogen doesn't know why she said that phrase. Father was speaking through her. It isn't what she intended at all. 'I mean, we can enjoy being here despite it not being real. Or even because we know it isn't real so there's nothing to worry about.'

Cate stands and turns in a circle to view the entire scene. Imogen places her headset back over her eyes and leans back on the sofa.

'It's amazing. Can you see it, too? The water wall?'

'That's a waterfall. Yes, isn't it marvellous!'

Imogen wondered as a girl how the water never ran out, how it fell forever in one direction just as the waves had eternal energy to keep lapping and the rain always returned after a dry spell. There's a slight glitch in the program as the water tumbles down, showing it's the same few frames on a loop.

'It feels really huge. But we're still at home.' Cate laughs as the swans take flight, honking across a blue sky.

That's exactly it. How could it be any more perfect than seeing a world that isn't demanding or unpredictable? To be with Cate in beautiful places from the safety of home. She wishes she'd thought of it before. An ideal compromise. They'd create their own world and never have to leave it.

17

———

CATE

The new family arrives at the holiday house while I'm out gathering snails for a race. It poured with rain this morning which meant they were all over the stone walls. Mam said it wasn't fair to make them race when they hadn't chosen to but I always ask their permission. I peek through the bushes and hold my breath as three people get out of a blue car – a mum, dad and a girl only a little shorter than me.

I knew it! I had wished it so very hard that maybe I made it come true. Or as I get older, I could be getting more of Mam's skills in seeing into different times: I'd predicted that this would be the year I get my first proper friend.

My friend has very straight black hair that shines. Her silver top ties around the back of her neck instead of having straps. She jumps around behind the car while her parents empty the boot. I think she has extra electricity like me. I can't hear what they're saying but my friend sounds excited and her dad puts his arm around her shoulders as they get to the front door where the mum opens up. They buzz in and out collecting items from the car. There is a sticker on the boot with the shape of Wales and a dragon. I know about that because it's part of the United

Kingdom. I like the sound of the kingdoms uniting after all those battles long ago. Mam said she's been to Wales which is a different country and has lots of small villages surrounded by the sea.

My friend is in *our* house. Our other house. I want to see which bedroom she's in but the sun bounces off the windows so I can't tell. She doesn't know that I made the beds, vacuumed the carpet and put little bowls of pine cones out that I'd soaked in lavender oil to make it smell lovely. We are already connected.

If I was back in the bedroom with the funny stacked beds, she could lie on the top one and dangle over to chat to me on the bottom one. She'd tell me about everything she saw on her way to Halham and I'd promise to show her the best parts of the village.

Her mother would make us hot chocolate and sing in Welsh. Her father would tell us about when he was the captain of a ship and travelled all the oceans.

I can't tell Mam I've seen them. I haven't yet dared to ask if I'm allowed to talk to visitors now that I'm older, so I run over to the playground to tell the elderly couple. Mister leans gently onto Missus at their usual spot by the side of the climbing frame. She doesn't take his weight but I think it helps him to know she's there just in case he ever starts to fall.

'My friend has arrived! Well, she's not my friend yet but I think she will be cos I wished it very hard. I got goose pimples when I saw her. That's when your skin tells you something is important.'

It's nice to have them to tell. Sometimes I get bored in my own mind and my words long to jump out of my mouth into the air. I can trust Mister and Missus. They both look much happier and healthier in the springtime than in cold winter. I used to jump up into Mister's arms when I was smaller. He's still solid despite his age. When I was little, I'd tell them about my bad dreams or sore fingers or what kind of colour Mam had been that day. But as I got bigger and they got older it didn't seem right to load them with heavy worries so now I try to be as cheery as I can.

'And I'll bring my friend to meet you, of course! You can watch us in the playground. She might do upside-down swinging if we help each other.'

I scoot round to Missus so she doesn't feel left out. She isn't much smaller than her husband but seems more delicate in her frame. The scent of her perfume is familiar and comforting. I lean against her middle, listening out for any hint of reply from inside. The couple stand so close to one another that the arms of their branches overlap, mixing her small dark leaves with his rounder, light ones.

'Anyway, I better get home now so I can plan what to do with my friend this week. See you later!' They wave their goodbyes in the wind.

I want to run all the way home but make myself walk fast instead so that Mam doesn't worry that another bad thing has happened.

There's a type of poem where you use each letter of a word to describe it. I try to make one about my friend. FRIEND.

F is for fun – the kind of thing that Mam isn't too keen on because she's a grown-up and says that I'm not little anymore.

R is for remembering – every new thing I do with my friend can go in my memory list so even when she's gone, I keep hold of her on the inside.

I is for interesting – I can tell her things that I've learnt from Mam which she may not already know, and she would have a million things to tell me about outside of Halham.

E is for excitement – I can already feel it in the roly-poly of my stomach.

N is for new – she can teach me new games and facts that don't belong to Mam.

And D. What is D for? Not desperate, not death, not destruction. D is a negative letter, I never noticed that before. D is for dilemma, deceit, dark. I'm nearly at the house and I can't get my poem right. I slow down so that I have a bit more time. I have an idea. In my mind, I add a colon in front of the D – :D – and now it's a smiling face which is what friendship is about.

Back in my bedroom, I'm unsure what to do that will help me clutch on to my happiness. I search through the drawers under my bed until I find my large notebook. I don't like writing very much but when I'm excited it postpones the pain. I sharpen my pencil so that it's the neatest it can be for page one of the script.

> CATE: Hi, I'm Cate, I live in Halham and I can show you all the best things about it. Also, I made your bedroom nice. Did you like it?
>
> FRIEND: Yes I love the room, thanks. It would be great to see Halham.
>
> THEY PLAY AND LAUGH.
>
> FRIEND: Would you like to know all about where I live?
>
> CATE: Oh yes.
>
> FRIEND: I'll tell you. It's a shame I can't show you things outside Halham because we are best friends.

If something is the best then it's number one. There can't be two bests because then that's not best anymore. I dive back into the drawer to look for my eraser but I can't find it.

> FRIEND: I'll tell you. It's a shame we can't see

more together ~~*because we are best friends*~~*. That would be extra fun and we could teach each other stuff.*
CATE: I know a secret way out of this garden.

Mam pushes open the door without knocking which makes me jump and drop my pencil.

'Well, I never thought I'd see it! Are you doing extra writing?'

I snap the notebook shut and keep my hand on top of it on the bed. 'I'm writing a play. It's secret.' I press my toes into the carpet and say *It's all right, it's all right* over and over in my head while Mam smiles at me.

'That's great, Cate.' She seems distracted, not using her usual Cateologist skills to figure out what I'm really doing. 'I'm off to buy a few things we need. The holiday family are here now. I'm sure they're very happy with what a good job you made of cleaning the place.'

'Okay, see you later.'

I don't know why I never realised before, but you can write whatever you want. It doesn't have to follow the rules. I'm so excited for the next line that I press down too hard and snap the point off the pencil.

18

IMOGEN

AGE 10

'I don't want to go back in,' Imogen whispered to Father as she tried to push past him to escape. She didn't want to spend a second longer in that room with the child who was far more ill than any they'd visited before on the Rounds. It was hard to tell the girl's age. She was already a skeleton. Her hair was sparse, her skin barely covering sharp bones.

Father gripped her shoulders tighter than usual. 'You absolutely will go back in. There is not an alternative decision to be made here. That poor child and her family are what matters.' He turned her body around as if she were his puppet. One nudge to her back and she was back in the room. There wasn't a choice.

Imogen didn't want to look at the girl. Her eye sockets looked deep and dangerous. Every time she breathed out there was a strange rattling noise. The smell in the room was putrid. The girl's mother sat at the end of the bed crying without sound. She had her hands clasped in prayer and rocked.

The girl's hand rested on the bed upturned; waiting to be held. Imogen tried her best to feel the same compassion as Father but all she felt was revulsion. She didn't want to be in the room when the girl died. She wanted to be back home lying in the bath with bubbles or riding her bike downhill with her feet off the pedals, enjoying the effortless freedom of descent.

She wanted to be a normal girl who didn't have to come into houses of death or have red-eyed parents howl at her in desperation. It must be clear to everyone that this girl was about to die. No magic or belief could stop it now. Not even the hand of God could clear out the girl's lungs or put meat back onto the bone.

Vomit forced its way into the back of Imogen's mouth. She swallowed its bitter message. Imogen pulled back but knew there was no way out of the room past Father who stood in the doorway on solemn guard duty.

It wasn't fair. She wanted her own life and her own decisions. She was double-digits now! She should have choice. Father only cared about the Rounds and all these strangers. He cared about that more than his own daughter.

That's when the red-hot lava of her anger and fear turned into something else. It blackened and hardened. Her rage became rock.

Imogen decided in that moment to take control. Her body wasn't hers to do as she wished but her mind was. She reached out to take hold of the child's hand. It was the same size as her own. She visualised that hand as belonging to a mannequin. The room became a stage full of life-size dolls. Medical equipment was a prop.

The audience held their breath awaiting a climax. Imogen closed her eyes and made her face look sad. But she would not let anything happen. No tingling. No rush of emotion. No search for the blackness within the child's blood and bone. Nothing special at all.

'Just a few more hours, I'm begging you.' Imogen let the mother's voice turn to music; discordant notes with no meaning.

'Her dad's on his way from the rig, please help her. She can't go without Jack here.' The melancholy tune played on but Imogen was barely listening.

Father responded in soothing bass note tones.

The child's hand was a dead weight. It was cold and dry. She needed to be careful not to heat it with her fury. *A stone is cold,* she told herself. She froze out her emotions and the spikes of fear from family who had gathered around her. She didn't belong here.

Imogen concentrated on transporting herself out of the room. Sometimes at the Rounds it happened without her intending it but never for long. Imogen usually brought herself back because Father told her that her touch would only work if she tried her very best and believed. She'd never tested out the alternative, until now.

Imogen focused hard behind her closed eyelids to send herself far away. Usually, the ideal place would be home. But that no longer felt like where she wanted to be. She knew exactly the right location to escape. The sand was warm between her toes which she wiggled to dig herself in further. Waves lapped in raspy rhythm. A seagull cried. In her palm rested a cold shell that once housed a beautiful creature. All that mattered was the in and out of her own breath, as endless as the ocean ahead of her. Nobody in the room knew that she wasn't with them, not wholly. She waited on the beach for twenty minutes until it was all over.

On their way home after the girl's death, Father had been unusually quiet. Imogen's victory of gaining control over herself crumbled. What had been the price?

'I don't understand, love. It's not your fault. But I don't understand why it didn't buy a little time. Did you feel the same as usual? Was something different this time?'

Imogen needed the right answer. Panic bubbled up. She'd

made a terrible mistake. What would happen if she and Father stopped the Rounds? Or if word got out that she was as useless as prayer?

'Yes, it felt different.'

Father drove on for another mile or two until they reached a place to pull in. That had given Imogen time to think. In the layby, Father unbuckled his seatbelt and turned to give Imogen his full attention.

'I know it's hard, but can you tell me about it?' The concern on Father's face was everything she needed. He was focused on her rather than the sick girl now.

'I tried but the tingling was different. Like she was pushing it away. She wanted to leave. I wanted to do the right thing.' How easy it was to lie when Father's face lit up to those words.

He nodded slowly as if readjusting the story that he told himself. 'That makes sense, she wanted peace. You did the right thing even though it was difficult. I'm proud of you.'

Imogen wanted to bask in the sweetness of Father's praise but couldn't quite keep hold of it. On the long journey home, it soured. He was pleased with her but it was still all about the Rounds and what she could do.

As they travelled through the night, Imogen's brain pulsed with painful questions. Had it been too late for the thin girl? Perhaps it would never have worked anyway. Or had she done a terrible thing by not trying and robbed a family of the chance to be together for a final time? She couldn't risk that again.

The truth of it was that she and Father had their roles to play and she mustn't change the rules again. If she didn't play her part and succeed, the two halves of them may no longer fit together.

19

CATE

It's been two days since my friend arrived. I need to find a way to get near to her. I'm doing a project about leaves which gives me a good reason for spending time close to the hedges and trees that surround the holiday house. I take a wicker basket balanced over my arm to collect specimens.

I peek through the leaves to check that the car is still parked up. The family hasn't gone anywhere so my friend must be in the house. To pass the time, I rearrange my leaves into size order, then spikiness order, and now from light green to dark green. I prick myself on the dark, sharp leaves on purpose. It stops me from drifting away. Mam is busy and if I wait long enough, then my friend will come out and I can start directing our play.

I think about how different it is out here to when we wore the headset. Touching crisp leaves is the kind of thing that doesn't work with a headset on. Your hand can't grab or feel or line things up. The world seems huge and just at the end of your arm but it's a kind of trick. It's a place that doesn't really exist apart from inside a computer.

After a while, I'd pulled the headset up a little and watched

Mam. She was smiling, moving her head from side to side. But really, she was facing a cupboard and sitting right next to me without seeing me. Mam says it's called virtual reality which I think means not-quite-real. That might be why she chose it for me. It's brilliant and awful at the same time, like being awake inside a dream.

There's a man's cough and some high-pitched laughter not far from where I'm sitting. My friend is out of the house! I don't want the family to think I'm a spying girl so I run to the playground. What if she goes in the other direction? I need her to come and see what's here. She'll love it.

The blackbird gives me an answer. He's perched on the top of a tree on the edge of the playground. He tilts his head one way then another. His yellow beak doesn't sing yet.

I squeeze myself through the metal bars of the climbing frame. The basket doesn't fit so I leave it just outside. The brown cardigan that was tied around my waist makes a soft base by my feet. I grab the leaves from the basket and let them fall in no order at all to build a small nest. The blackbird switches position to a bush nearby to get a better view.

'I need your best calling song to get my friend to come over, please.' He flutters his wings in reply. 'I'll start, if you like?'

I close my eyes to help the music come. I know the blackbird is watching and waiting. I start with a whistle. I can't do the trill easily so change to singing. The notes vibrate in the back of my mouth. My blackbird replies. I knew he would. The spell works best when we sing together. I let him finish then I sing back. I'm not sure how far away my friend is but I think I have to keep my eyes closed for it to work. I go back to whistling but it's not loud enough. I reach out until my fingertips touch the metal bars of the climbing frame. I tip my head back the same way that the blackbird does when he's calling across the field. This time I sing the loudest I ever have. There are no human words, only bird sounds. Vowels and high-pitched squeaks and warbling. He sings back to tell me it's working. I can't stop now. With each new line, I turn a little to make sure my call travels as far as it needs to. This time the blackbird doesn't answer. I open my eyes.

The magic worked. My friend is standing on the edge of the playground with her dad. She has black, shiny hair like bird feathers. A T-shirt as yellow as a beak. I glance at the nearby trees and bushes but the blackbird is nowhere to be seen.

My friend's dad squashes his lips together so tightly that they almost disappear altogether. He's holding his daughter's hand. I bet it feels nice.

'We were just taking a look around, if that's okay?'

Why is a grown-up asking me if he's allowed to walk in the village? My friend shuffles her weight from one foot to the other. She's wearing strange shoes that only have two bits of material that wedge between her toes. Her T-shirt is so short that her belly shows. She wears shorts that look like jeans which have been chopped really small. I must chop my jeans the same when I get back to my bedroom.

'Yes, this is the playground. I'm Cate, which is also Catelyn.' I glance down at the nest but feel a bit shy now. Should I explain about the blackbird? Do Outsiders know how to talk to animals? 'The swing tyre is the best. You can go on it as long as you like. I could push it.' I nudge my head towards it.

'Right. Well, I'm sure Alana would love a turn. I was going to nip to the shop for a few things. Is there one that's walkable from here?'

Alana! What a wonderful name. It's the sound of a sigh you make when you lie on your back in the sun and it warms your face to just the right temperature.

'The corner shop is just over there, with the red door. You have to shove it with your shoulder because it's a bit stiff but there's everything you need in there.' I want to tell them all the good things about Halham to make sure they love it as much as me but I must remember to take turns when talking.

Alana's dad looks unsure if he should go or not. I really want him to leave so I can speak with my friend. We need time to learn about each other and I'm not sure that having a grown-up around is a good idea. He looks like the kind of grown-up that has anxiety atoms. I don't think he's sure about leaving Alana here. He probably doesn't know that it's the safest village in England. Maybe I'm being weird. I try to think what normal people say like when Mam chats to Farmer Grove.

'Looks like a good day for it.' I'm not sure what the 'it' is but I nod my head and look across at the fields then up to the sky in the same way Mam does.

Alana is checking out one item in the playground to the next. I suddenly feel hot and sweaty about what will happen if she asks me about the nest. It can be hard to put things into words when they come from a feeling of what I must do, like I'm following orders from someone who whispers in my ear.

'Dad, can I come and choose some sweets? I'll share them with Catelyn.'

My breath is sucked right out of my lungs with happiness. She wants to share with me, her new friend. And she called me Catelyn. It sounds strange and thrilling. My entire body hums in a pleasant tingle.

'Come on then.'

Alana's dad leads the way and she grins at me. We walk next to each other and it's like my feet have forgotten how to go one in front of the other in a straight line. She's so close to me. I start to skip instead and Alana copies me. She can skip really high. I do the same and we giggle as we bounce along the path. I will call this memory 'skipping with my friend' and put it straight into the top five happy memories list.

When we get to the corner shop, I want to please Alana's dad so I offer to nudge the door open. It's easy when you know the right place to shove. The shelves are full with tins, bottles, huge bags of cereal and rice, and bottles of squash. Alana and her dad seem surprised at how much there is.

'I know where the treats are.' I reach down to the box in the corner where there are boxes of liquorice that Mam loves and the marshmallow treats that we toasted over a fire in the winter. I hand a bag over to Alana hoping she likes the pink ones so I can eat the white ones that I prefer. Her dad stays near the door.

'Ahh, this isn't what I meant. I need a proper shop to get milk, teabags, cold meat for our sandwiches.'

It hurts a little that he doesn't think our corner shop is good enough. Perhaps he lives in a bigger village or even a huge city.

'Mam can bring you some milk over from the farm. You can take what you want from the corner shop as long as you use it, that's the rule.'

Alana runs her finger along the shelf with pasta and sauces.

'It looks like I'll need to take a drive then. It wouldn't be right to take from your family's food store, I've money to get what we need.'

I don't understand what he means. There are some delivery boxes that haven't been cut open yet. The address label states that they're for Halham.

'It's okay, look here, it's for all of us. The food is for everyone in the village like it says.'

Alana's dad backs out of the corner shop and she follows. He raises his hand over his eyes which helps him see further down the track.

'Well, I'll get the car and nip into the village and get what we need. Alana, do you want to come with me?'

I hold my breath. It doesn't make any sense. He's already in the village. Where's he going to? *It doesn't matter if you don't like the corner shop just please let me keep my friend.*

Alana shakes her head and pops another marshmallow into her mouth. 'I want to go on the swing.'

'Okay, stay at the swings till I'm back. And be kind and helpful to your new friend.' He turns to me then and his voice goes all funny like he's talking to a lamb. 'Is it okay for you to play out? Will your mummy be worrying about you? Alana is a big girl, she'll look after you, my love.'

I can hardly enjoy him calling me 'my love' because I don't understand why Alana would need to look after me in my own village or why he changed his voice when he spoke to me. I think it's something to do with the corner shop but I can't figure out what. I don't want to cry, so I smile and look away.

'Can we have fish and chips for lunch, Dad. Please?' Her bottom lip pouts down a little. Her dad kisses her on the top of the head. He gets his phone out of his pocket and moves his finger about. Maybe all phones except Mam's can give answers.

'There's a fish and chip shop not too far away. Go on then, seeing as we're on holiday.' Our corner shop doesn't have fish or chips in it but it does have sacks of potatoes.

'Is it a nice one, Catelyn? Why don't you come with us?'

Outside the village. Not far away. A shop that only sells chips and fish. Are the fish in tanks and you choose one to eat with your chips? I don't really like the sound of that but it's fascinating.

This is my chance. Why don't I feel happy? Why am I not racing Alana to her car to find out what it's like to sit in one that's moving? I could see the next village. Find out what lies beyond the fields. Have a special time with my friend.

The woodlice disagree. They flood into the back of my throat to clog up my airway so I can't talk. They wriggle their cruel legs over my eyeballs so I can't see properly. They cram themselves through my left ventricle, pushing outwards so my heart feels like it's going to explode. The pull to stay is stronger than the push to leave Halham.

'I'm going on the swing, see you later,' I shout over my shoulder as I run. My legs don't work properly so I almost trip over. I'm sick. I'm homesick.

I close my eyes on the tyre swing. Up, down, up, down, up, down. The rocking rhythm calms my body down with each turn forwards and back. He said Halham isn't a village. That the corner shop isn't a shop. People use words differently. What does that stupid man know who's an Outsider? He doesn't understand. Mam said it was better being just me and her. I keep going, forwards and backwards with my eyes tightly shut.

Mam used to get homesick. That's when you miss your house or village so much that you feel poorly. She said I never had to feel homesick like that because I'm always at home. I lean back and make the tyre swing higher. So why do I still feel like I'm missing a place? I bend my legs up and down until they hurt. All the sadness runs from my brain into my bones. It gathers in my thighs and burns.

20

IMOGEN

NOW

Cate seemed agitated and bursting with hormones so Imogen slipped out to meet Zach in the access road. The camper-van feels bigger on the inside than it appeared from the outside. They sit opposite one another on velvet-covered benches. Imogen tries not to imagine the seats being flattened into a double bed. The back window looks out onto the yellow fields over the road, perfect against a blue-sky morning.

Zach takes Imogen's hand. She pulls back slightly at the unfamiliarity of touch before letting her wrist loosen in his grasp.

'How on earth have you managed this all by yourself for so long?'

He doesn't realise yet that this is exactly what Imogen wanted: her and Cate in their own bubble, protected from demands and expectations. There hadn't been an alternative.

'It was tough at first.'

How could she begin to explain those early years? Imogen's vision of herself as a playful, contented mother was destroyed by how overwhelmed she was. There'd been too much; too much to plan, too much responsibility, too much of the desperate, painful cries of a baby that never seemed satiated. She hadn't expected to be such a complete failure.

After years of being treated as if she was special, Imogen was thrust into an adult life where she was an ordinary disappointment. Her battery could no longer be charged by the grateful awe of strangers or the approval of Father. That toxic reliance took its toll. Without the mirror of others' approval, her bones turned to metal rods, her organs became cogs, her daily tasks were a day's programme to be completed. She'd stare at her beautiful girl and feel absolutely nothing.

'Could you tell me about Cate? Is she like you?' Zach squeezes Imogen's hand slightly. Perhaps he imagines an impossible future with all three of them together.

'She is one hundred per cent her own person, I can assure you of that! If she was in here with us now, she'd be teaching us a birdsong for a species we'd failed to notice that was just about visible through those doors. Or finding fascination in the material of these bench cushions, running her finger along and telling you what the colours feel like inside her. Or asking you about any famous Zachs in history so she could draw one for you. Actually, she'd love the fact that you can draw. I bet she'd watch and try to copy your movements.'

Imogen allows herself this selfish portrayal of a family life that can never become real. She'd never thought about any similarities between the two of them before this moment.

'Oh, she is clumsy like me though. And she loves Halham fiercely. She's happy here.' Imogen needs to build an idyllic picture for Zach. It will be hard for him to understand from the outside. That's what he is now, an Outsider. She pulls her hands away and rests them on her lap. Over the years, Imogen has learnt to recharge her own batteries. There are practical reasons to have Zach involved. She mustn't let herself soften again.

'Does she know about me?'

Zach asks gently but there's tension in the air between them.

Imogen shakes her head and studies the lines on her palms; a strong life line, a feathered heart line that fractures and fades.

'I'd like to meet her, you understand that, don't you?'

It seems that Zach doesn't have another family. Or at least, he doesn't have other children. Imogen can't imagine what kind of life Zach has formed for himself so far away. He lives by the sea as they had dreamt of together. He doesn't wear a ring but that doesn't mean much these days.

'It's complicated. I want her to meet you first without any expectation.'

That wasn't quite right. The discomfort that gnawed at Imogen was uglier than protection of her daughter. She'd struggled to get to sleep the night before while pulling the covers off different parts of her body. An irritation wouldn't leave her. She pictured Zach and Cate sitting cross-legged together in the field, as if she was watching from far away. How they may recognise something in each other as familiar despite the distance of time and space that had kept them apart. They shared a playfulness that Imogen had always needed to wear as a costume. She realised that the high stakes were not only about Zach disagreeing with her parenting; she was afraid that Cate may prefer him to her.

'I don't want her to feel tricked by me. I can't be one thing and then another.'

Imogen wants to ask something impossible; can Zach play a role and never reveal himself as birth father? She'd intended to explain the basics of the life cycle before Cate reached puberty. They live by a farm, an ideal way to teach about reproduction and inherited genes. She'd avoided it. There never seemed to be a right time.

'I hadn't expected to hear from you after so long. You

stopped trying after a year, so...' Imogen shrugs. She knows she's being unfair but she needs to claw back some control over the situation.

Zach slows down his speech as if trying to hold himself back. They dance dangerously close to a decade of hurt erupting.

'Well, if you'd spoken to me in a way that wasn't cold, or if you'd told me that you had a baby, I would have been back in a heartbeat. I didn't get to make that choice. You did.'

Imogen pushes her hands as hard as she can against the edge of the table that separates them.

When Cate was tiny, Imogen couldn't keep her eyes off her. There had been nobody to share those moments with. The cooing sounds she made, fascinated by her own fists. A zombie crawl with Cate's look of surprise as she moved backwards rather than forwards, even further from the toy duck she wanted to grasp. Early vocalisations dancing so beautifully close to Mama; long conversations with turn-taking that made no sense at all yet were her main source of human interaction day to day.

'I can give you one of the photographs to keep. Once she's eighteen it will be different.'

Zach sighs. She's made a mistake allowing him here. He doesn't understand.

'I don't think that's fair on any of us. Imogen, I'm here now. I want to meet her and you may find she wants to meet me. It doesn't have to be today, of course not. But please don't make this choice for her. Or me.'

The hurt on Zach's face reaches through the cracks in Imogen's armour. It tries to bring back images from that dreadful night; his fear and regret.

'Okay, but not now. Please let me do this my own way. I know her. She can become overwhelmed easily. Trust me with this, please.'

Imogen could only hope that Zach would believe she knew what was best. It was hard enough arguing with her own mind without having to do it with another person.

Zach leans back. They can tread carefully around the truth for a while longer.

'I've been so wrapped up in everything to do with Cate that I haven't even asked how you are or what you've been doing all these years.'

Zach shrugs his answer and Imogen is relieved. None of that matters.

'We haven't talked about what happened that night with your father.'

Imogen knows these are the final moments that she and Zach will be together with any semblance to their past selves. There is so much to explain that she can't figure out any clear, concise way to do so. Her story would start with Once Upon a Time and take hours to tell. Those traditional ways to learn about human nature have long gone. Zach would interrupt her, make inferences, leap to action before she'd had a chance to complete one chapter. She lives in the wrong century.

'Not now. Not yet. Please?'

'I'll stay here for a little while then.'

They lock eyes and Imogen can still see the boy she adored and a hundred paths of possibility between them that were never taken.

There are experiences that can't be expressed adequately by words; description moulds them into the wrong shape. Sometimes only action suffices. She can't help but move towards him. The pull is instinctive. She holds Zach's face. They are forever together and apart.

21

CATE

Mam told me a big lie. Now she's told me the truth. I think I preferred the lie.

The man-smell wasn't a delivery man. I knew it! Mam lays out two cheese scones each on the picnic table in our garden. We've never had more than one each at a time before. She hadn't asked me to help with making them so they were perfectly round instead of lumpy shapes like when I do it.

'I think it's essential that we can trust one another, so I want to apologise for telling you something that wasn't true the other day. I was caught off guard and hadn't yet had a chance to think about the way to discuss it with you.'

I take a bite of the scone even though my mouth doesn't want it so that I don't interrupt.

'You're so observant I should have guessed you would catch Zach's scent. That's who visited. It's a man I knew a long time ago. He came to see me and he's staying nearby.'

Mam told me once that there's a phrase called "letting the cat out of the bag", which is when a secret escapes a sack that you'd tied it up tight in. In the olden days, someone could sell you a wriggly pig for lots of money. When you got home and opened it, there was no pig, just a cat. Imagine how cross a farmer would be. A cat would stride away and do whatever it wanted. Not much use when all you needed was a pig. I think about Mam's sack. Something has been wriggling about in it for days, I could tell. The lilac dress wasn't for me. It was for a man.

It would be good to float away right now. But my water won't come. Instead, there are sharp pains in my chest as if a gardening fork has been stuck straight through me. It has made holes that Mam looks through.

'You could have said a friend came to visit. What's so hard about that?' What's so *secret* about that, unless there's something really bad that Mam was trying to cover up?

Mam picks crumbs from her scone. She hasn't eaten anything. Her cheeks are flushed red. 'I know I don't talk very much about when I was younger. I had to really think hard about whether it was in your best interests.' Her eyes go watery which I don't like at all. I mustn't let her sadness come back. The Outsider, Zach, could make things go wrong between us. I won't let him.

'It's fine. I know.'

'Well, perhaps I should explain a little more, now that you're getting older.'

I can't help it. I have to ask. It's in my top three questions and I might not get such an obvious chance again. 'How old am I?'

Mam lets go of the scone and stares at me. She places her palms flat on the table. I can imagine the cool, grainy wood as if her hands are my hands. I like it when we feel like the same person. Maybe I can make her answer if I say numbers in my head. *Ten, eleven, twelve, thirteen, fourteen, fifteen.*

'You're thirteen. That means you're a teenager. You know in German they call this period *Sturm und Drang* – which means storm and stress – but it doesn't need to be like that. We can still be happy at home. You're a growing girl and on your way to becoming a wonderful woman, which is all that I could ask for.'

It's hard to concentrate on what Mam is saying after she reveals that I'm thirteen years old. It's an actual number that belongs to me. I'm a teenager; nearly a woman. Under the table I count on my fingers that I have five years left until I'm a grown-up.

You'd think that having a question answered would be like having a long, cool drink of water when you've been out in the fields sweating for hours. But instead of relief, that one question sprouts many more. They grow outwards in all directions like the roots of a dandelion: stubborn, resilient, finding new places to push through hard surfaces.

Mam has already revealed more than ever before. She may tell me more as long as I don't push too hard. It's hard to control myself. So I just say 'Zach?' and shove the second scone into my mouth where it absorbs the last bit of my saliva.

Before Mam answers, I notice the flash of a smile swipes the corners of her mouth up. She pushes it away but it's too late. I think I know another secret. Mam and Zach are like Brown and his friend. That's different to BFF. It's kissing and grunts and nobody else matters.

I need to get rid of him. But I mustn't let Mam know what I've figured out. She doesn't want storm and stress.

'He has a special kind of van for camping that he sleeps in. Actually, I think you'd love it. Zach would really like to meet you.'

I don't care about what he'd like. She does the kind of swallow that is called a gulp in stories. It's very important to her that I meet him but also she's worried about it. She becomes a Cateologist again. I'm going to be the best specimen for her to observe; a beautiful creature that has turned to stone and will always look the same.

'Can I see Zach's van when I meet him? We could make some cupcakes. I could put his favourite animal on the top, what is it?'

Mam laughs and I can see she's thrilled. She wants Zach to feel special. Maybe more special than me. It feels like she's reached over the table and is slowly turning the gardening fork that is in my torso. It tears through my organs, slicing my intestines, gall bladder, liver and kidneys.

'What a lovely idea, Cate. That's an easy one, his favourite animal is a dog. He would stop at every dog we met, no matter what the breed or size. And they loved him, too. Fierce-looking rottweilers or yappy, tiny dogs, even those ones with the squashed-up faces.'

Mam is smiling into the past. She's slipping further away from me. Dogs love him so much because they have something in common. All dogs are descended from the grey wolf. That's what Zach is – a wolf at the door. Mam is under some kind of spell. She doesn't even think about the phrase she taught me about bad people – "a wolf in sheep's clothing". That's a bad person who pretends they're sweet and the same as the rest of the herd. I sniffed him out though.

'I'll need time to make the cupcakes. When are we seeing him?' How long do I have to make a plan? I've got to get rid of him and save Mam.

'I suggested this afternoon. Why don't you nip to the corner shop and get some extra ingredients? We have eggs and flour. Grab some icing sugar and some ginger.'

I remember what Alana's dad said. It's risky to keep asking questions but it feels like I'm running out of time. 'Is it really a shop?'

Mam becomes very still.

I don't want her to find out that I've spoken with Alana. We haven't even had a chance to play together yet. I figured something out last night and can't believe I didn't think of it before. 'Remember the toy till I had when I was little and I liked to practise sums on it? We used the plastic coins for songs, like *the king was in his counting house, counting out his money*, and *one a penny, two a penny, hot cross buns*. But if the corner shop is a real shop, why don't we use money?'

Mam nods slowly. She's thinking hard. 'Yes of course, I remember that. We like to have our own names for some things, don't we? It's the way we make things our own. I called it the *corner shop* because it was so like a shop. An Outsider might call it a store room or outhouse. That's not as fun, though.'

That could be true. I want it to be true. But Mam's fingers pinch the material of her trousers and her foot taps the floor. She's wriggly because she's trying to stop the truth from spilling out. If this was a game of cards, Mam would be trying to hide that she had high points or all the queens. She's a liar.

'Okay, I'll go and fetch what we need.' I slip off my chair and head out to the door to escape before Mam can read what's behind my eyes. She probably has her own secrets that she wants to return to. That gives me an idea. 'Mam, can I make the cupcakes myself this time? You can go and get your jobs done before we meet Zach.'

I want her to say no, so things stay the same. I want her to say yes, so I can find out what she does without me. That's what Mam would call win-win because whatever happens, you get something you want. But I think it might be lose-lose.

'If you're sure, then yes. I'll pop back to check if you need any help later. Don't forget to wear the oven gloves before you pull the hot shelf out.'

Mam does care about me, or else she wouldn't warn me about getting burnt. But she doesn't care enough to stay with me or tell Zach that we don't need anybody else. I take my time as I walk down the path to what isn't a corner shop.

Everything is changing at Halham. It's becoming a world of opposites.

I grab what I need and take it back to the house, laying the ingredients out in a line. Is this the kind of thing a thirteen-year-old does? I stir the mixture with my right hand. That's the one that has been outside of the village. Alana's dad said that Halham isn't a village. We have a book made from old photographs called *One Hundred Historic Villages in England*. They are black and white. Some show children who wear frilly, white dresses or caps. There are horses being led by men wearing hats. Some of the buildings look like the ones at the end of Halham, with thatched roofs and stone walls.

None of the pictures show any kind of gate. And our village gates are shiny metal not old, wooden gates like the ones that divide the fields. I asked Mam once about the village gates.

'I don't think they had gates into Halham in the olden days.'

Mam hadn't looked up from the paper she was writing on. 'We're lucky to benefit from technology. Our gates work without us having to go outside in all kinds of weather because they are controlled remotely.'

I wanted to ask about the people who rattled and banged. I heard shouting one morning while I was doing cartwheels behind the house. I saw a lady leaning on a stick with a bandage on her head and an older woman who was shouting for us to let them in. They were Outsiders. Mam called me back in and put on some of her music so we couldn't hear the shouting. I felt a bit sorry for the lady with a poorly leg and head. I worried that she might have thought I was showing off by doing cartwheels in front of her. They didn't look like the kind of Outsiders that would be dangerous.

'I was wondering about the lady with the stick.' I hadn't wanted to upset Mam. *Wondering* is a good word because it just means you've been thinking about something and it doesn't say that the other person is wrong. Mam is never wrong because she's a grown-up but I'd wanted her to explain it to me. 'I mean, I know she didn't need to come into Halham but it looked like she really wanted to. And the gates stopped her having a quick look.'

Mam plonked her pen down and sighed. 'It's called a gated community. That means, Halham is not for Outsiders. They don't belong here. They want to take things that don't belong to them. We have nothing to give to them. We have the right to privacy and freedom, don't you think?' I nodded my agreement but that didn't stop Mam giving me the full talk. 'Imagine if we went around knocking on people's doors, expecting to be let into their house any time of day or night. We'd have no right unless we were invited.'

That made sense. Except we were never invited anywhere.

I'd forgotten all about our conversation, filed it away to keep things simple and happy at Halham. What else have I filed away?

I try to spoon equal amounts of mixture into each paper case. My hands are still a little bit shaky. I don't know what the woman with the stick wanted to see or take from Halham. How come Zach is allowed in? He's not paying for the holiday house. What does he want to see or take?

Is it Mam?

I put the oven on to warm up but don't put the cupcakes in yet. This is my chance to find out what I can before I meet Zach later. I close my eyes and press my palms onto my eyeballs which makes shapes and colours show up. If I concentrate really hard, I might be able to see where Mam is. I need to become part of her. We are the same. We only need each other. I'm here in my body and there in her body.

I know where she is.

22

IMOGEN

AGE 17

It was Imogen's seventeenth birthday; she was finally on the countdown to freedom. She'd been told her whole life that everything would change when she turned eighteen.

It used to scare her. She'd been fearful of the impact on her special relationship with Father. If they couldn't do the Rounds, would he drift away from her, immersing himself more and more into his books? Father had always said that her healing powers were attached to childhood. They would no longer work once she was an adult. He'd promised her a special gift at eighteen to mark the end of the Rounds.

Since she met Zach, she feared less about the change with Father. The greatest gift would be release from her obligations.

In the previous year or so, Imogen realised that Father had become better off financially. She'd never queried how they funded their lifestyle without him going out to work. They had no contact with her mother. The old ladies they visited couldn't have had much money to pay for visits. Perhaps he'd been added to wills that were starting to pay out? She never told Father what she had discovered in The Blacksmith's Cottage. Putting a price to it made her queasy.

What mattered now was the countdown. One year to go. Imogen wondered about the precision of it all. Babies were rarely born on their due date and some cultures classed birthdays in an altogether different way such as the Koreans whose age changed on the first of January.

Perhaps it didn't matter at all. The Rounds would end on the day she turned seventeen years, 364 days old. Her life would become hers. Any financial gain was a bonus. It was owed to her. But a life without responsibility would be the real gift. If the sum of money was large enough, she and Zach could buy their own place far away from Halham with a sea view.

'Are you going out, then? Leaving your old dad?'

It was strange as not so long ago, Imogen's dream birthday would have been to have Father all to herself. He knew about Zach but she kept the description of her birthday plans vague. It had never felt comfortable to talk about her boyfriend. There was an unspoken recognition from Father than he was no longer the only person who mattered in Imogen's life.

'There's plenty of food left for your supper. Don't wait up, I'm going into town.'

'I'll be fine here. You know, I will always be here; Halham is part of me. Don't go putting me in some nursing home one day. I'll take my last breath where I belong. But there's far more for me to do before that day comes along.' Father patted the dining-room chair next to him in expectation.

Imogen's phone buzzed with messages in her pocket. Zach was on his way in the taxi already. She didn't want to be in the house any longer. Its faded décor and mismatched furniture felt old and oppressive – a far cry from the minimalist homes she scrolled through online. The lack of redecorating was another way in which Father trapped them in the loop of sameness. One day she'd live in a flat with only glass, metal and reclaimed wood. Every item in it would be digitally controlled. There'd be so much light that it would feel like living outdoors.

'I've got to finish getting ready.'

He followed Imogen out to the hallway with the devoted agitation of a dog that knows its owner is going to leave the house soon without it. Imogen thought she would relish the tables turning but in reality, it left her feeling deflated. She wanted to see Father's strength back so they could both move on to the next parts of their lives. This pathetic shadow of the man he used to be only furthered her determination to escape in exactly one year. His trotting after her made her hands itch to push him away from her. She was suffocating.

'It's good to see you enjoying yourself. Your years of service have changed many lives for the better. That's why the important work must continue, Immy, surely you can see that?'

Imogen was curling the ends of her hair with hot tongs in preparation for a meal out with Zach. It was rare for them to do anything in town but Father had been so generous with birthday money this year that she planned to pay for a taxi. She hadn't been brave enough to book a hotel; that would have involved a conversation with Father she wasn't ready for.

'I know it's important to you but I only have one year left. It won't work after my next birthday, so there's no point talking about it.' Imogen tilted her head one way and then the other in the hallway mirror. The cottage didn't allow much natural light in so it was hard to tell if her foundation was even. She didn't usually wear much make-up but wanted the night to be special. Each eyelid was swept with glittery bronze powder and eyeliner ticked up from the corners. 'It doesn't have to all stop for you. There are plenty of ways you could still meet and talk with people. You always make them feel better with the things you say.'

She watched Father's mirror image. He seemed to have aged

these last two years, as if he was already winding down for the loss of his role. Imogen shook her shoulders as if that could shake off the feelings of responsibility for him.

'The Rounds must continue. You know that in your heart. And only you can make that happen.'

It was unthinkable that turning eighteen wouldn't be the end of the Rounds. The message had been clear her whole life – at eighteen it would all stop permanently. His voice didn't sound right. There was a pleading undertone that replaced his usual directness.

Imogen blocked out whatever tried to creep up from the centre of her. She wouldn't let the day be ruined. 'Can we talk about this later; I need to finish getting ready. My taxi will be here soon.'

He stepped closer to her but Imogen didn't turn around. The mirror was her protection. The back-to-front version of her Father seemed unfamiliar, like an uncle who couldn't replace his deceased brother no matter how hard he tried.

'It's the female family line; from my grandmother, to my mother, to you. A line that mustn't be broken.'

Imogen's body understood before she'd consciously caught up with the implications. A cold wave shuddered through her. She turned and crossed her arms in protection. Father never let up when he believed he was in the right. He'd been waiting for her birthday. Now the countdown began.

'I don't know what you mean. This isn't the right time.' She didn't want Father to say another word. She didn't want his hand to move towards her and settle on her stomach. She didn't want to realise the freedom he'd promised her at eighteen came at the expense of somebody else; somebody brand new.

'It's what our family does. You know that. It's a gift to the world.' He held his hand on her stomach and smiled while looking through her. In his mind, she was already replaced. 'You need to have a daughter as soon as possible. That's the right thing to do for all those people who need healing.'

Imogen felt nauseous. Why hadn't she seen this coming? It was never going to end. The promise of freedom was a curse. Her hand was shaky as she attempted to style her hair. 'I can't, won't. I've got to go now.'

Father blocked her path to the front door. 'You deserve your freedom. I would never dream of stopping that. You can do all the things you've been waiting for. I'd look after the little one. We'd be out of your way most days.'

He was already living in that future of doing the Rounds with a gurgling baby again. Strangers reaching out to hold a foot, stroke downy hair, suck up whatever they could no matter what impact that had on the infant or the rest of her life. New life as a means to an end. That's what she had been; a vessel, a project, a calling.

'Listen carefully. I love you. The Rounds have been important to both of us. But that's never, ever going to happen.'

Imogen pushed Father aside and grabbed her bag. She slammed the front door then ran down the path to meet Zach as if that was a means of escape, when she knew in reality it was only a pause on the inevitable.

23

CATE

Mam's contaminated. I understand now. That bad man Zach has touched her and now his germs are inside her. They're making her act weird. I think back to my farm worksheets. One way to identify sick animals on the farm is *prolonged lying duration and reduced feeding duration*. That's exactly Mam: more lying, less eating. His nasty infection is changing her and it could get worse if she spends more time with him. Mam has helped and protected me all of my life. Now it's my time to save her, even if she doesn't realise that she needs help.

My ballerina pumps are soft on the ground as I take the long route pressed flat against the hedgerow to get to Zach's van. It's light blue and white. I squeeze my eyes to see a bit further and wish I'd brought my binoculars. There's nobody sitting in the front but Mam said it has a kind of little room in the back. That's where she is. I'm so close to the edge of the path that the left side of my foot drops down and makes my ankle shout out in pain. I press my palm flat against my mouth so it doesn't shout too.

This is all stupid Zach's fault. I rub my ankle as fast as I can to confuse the nerve endings. They talk to your brain to say *pain, pain,* and if you rub them fast enough it mixes the letters up so the brain doesn't know what they're trying to say and it won't hurt so much. I know how to walk with my weight more on one leg and not even get wobbly because I've practised that.

The music that pours from the van isn't like anything I've heard before. There's a man saying poetry over the top of drums. He speaks so fast it's hard to catch the words but the lines almost rhyme. The rhythm of his words is sometimes off the beat which is called syncopation when an instrument does it.

He says some bad swear words that I heard Mam shout when a fox got into the chickens. We'd slept through it all. By the morning, it was too late. I dreamt of sticky blood on feathers for weeks afterwards. Mam gave the rest of the chickens away. The water pipes hummed for a long time from her shower room. She didn't speak the rest of the day.

It makes me remember the blood hiding now on a pad in my pants – the metallic, heavy scent of it. I don't know why I ever thought blood was like red water; pure and life-giving. It's lumpy, ugly stuff that darkens and smells of death.

I run my finger along the cool surface of the van as I walk past it. At the back is a rectangular window. If I peek in, I should be able to see Mam and Zach. Maybe they are kissing. Maybe they are fighting. Maybe the engine will start and they'll drive off from Halham and never come back. I close my eyes and crouch down in the grass at the side of the road.

There's a thing called quantum physics. Mam tried to explain but she didn't really understand it and had to read from a sheet. It's the teeniest, tiniest particles that exist. They are magical. One particle can be here and not here, or here and over there, at the same time. And it only decides where it is when you look at it.

I let the tiny quantum particles swirl around me. *The act of observation influences the thing being observed. The cat is both alive and dead.*

Mam is kissing.

And Mam is fighting.

And Mam is leaving me.

And Mam is home, icing the cupcakes that have cooled.

All of those could be true until I open my eyes and observe. If I stay here long enough, I can stop the certainty of the wrong thing happening. I roll off my sore ankle to sit on the grass. A different man chants to the music now. His voice is deep. There are sounds I've never heard before but are somehow familiar, as if I heard them before I was even born. He says *j'adore* which I know is French for "I love". The *r* sounds like a lion purring. It's a sign. In olden times, Mam's family were from France. She lost the language but says the sounds of her grandmother still live inside her. The past communicates with us all the time, we just have to know how to listen. The pain in my ankle has transformed. It throbs along to the beat of the music. There is only me and the music now. I try to catch the words I recognise from the opening of my dictionary as they float past me. *Argent*: silver, money. *Arrêter*: to stop, to stay, to put an end to. *Attraper*: to trap, to trick, to secure – like Mam wanted to with the fox but it got away. The words line up behind my eyelids into a poem of my own. *Poetry is a way to say the unsayable.*

'Cate?'

It's him. Zach isn't much taller than Mam. He looks at me in a weird way as if I'm covered in blood and feathers. I might have been saying my French poem out loud, I'm not sure. My face flushes with heat. I was supposed to spy on him, not the other way around.

'I need to speak to Mam.' I want to shout out to her but my throat feels tight. I can't see in the rear window. Zach presses a button on his phone and the music stops.

'Shall I call her for you? I wasn't expecting you both until later today.' His body is twitchy like when I'm trying to stop my electricity from making me move too much.

Mam isn't here. I was so sure but I got it wrong. Unless he's lying and she's tied up in his van or hiding from me on the back seat. *Attraper* – is Mam trapped or is she part of the trick on me? I don't know what to say and without the music to sing to, the pain has come back into my ankle.

'My foot.'

Zach gets closer and I realise the bad thing could happen again so I hold my arm out to stop him. He stays just out of reach but kneels down and is staring at my ankle. It's darkening and slightly swollen on the left side.

'This used to happen to Imogen all the time.' He glances up at me. 'All those aches and pains in her joints. She didn't complain really, she was always very strong. Seems like you're two peas in a pod.'

Mam had the same pains as me? I've tried so hard to hide the hurts but she knew what it felt like all along. Zach is right that Mam is strong. But he's tried to weaken her with his poison. I want to be cross. I want to be red-hot and get him far away from here but I also want to hear more about Mam when she was young. I can't keep the red inside. It's softening into pink. That might be exactly what he wants.

I tell my insects to stand on guard. The woodlice gather with their hard shells facing outwards to protect my body from his germs or charm. *You can't trust men.* I'm not sure the woodlice are up to the job with their squishy undersides. It would be better if they were very tiny armadillos.

'Woodlice are a bit like armadillos,' I say, making conversation to give me time to think what to do next.

Zach nods as if he was just thinking the same thing. 'You know, they really love armadillos in Texas. You see them on everything – caps, T-shirts, key rings. That armour on their back is made of bone. I saw the skeleton of one in the Natural History Museum in Washington. Really weird and amazing.'

'You've been to the United States of America?' That's on the other side of the world, across the Atlantic Ocean. There's a little smile on Zach's face and I'm not sure if that's because he's happy thinking about armadillos or if he's trying not to laugh at me. 'Did you go on a boat or an aeroplane?' I do a quick check of the skies for any aeroplanes and realise I've forgotten to pay attention to them recently. Is it my fault that Zach is here? Did a pilot see me and report it?

'It's a really long way, so I went on a plane. In fact, the US is so big, that you go on planes just to get from one city to another. It makes you realise how small the UK is. What's the furthest you've been with your mum?' Zach ties the white lace of his trainer even though it wasn't undone. I know what he's doing. He's trying to act like he isn't too interested in my answer. I know all these tricks.

'We have everything we need in Halham. Can you tell Mam to come now, please?'

Zach doesn't move. He's staring at me like he's trying to remember all the details for later. I wish I could tell what was happening behind his eyes but he's pulled down a thick curtain and it stops my guesses. He types into his phone. That must be how Mam and Zach have kept in touch for my whole life.

'I know somebody whose daughter has the same thing as you and Imogen. It's called hypermobility syndrome. It means you're extra stretchy and so your ligaments can't hold you properly and it can cause pain. That's why you fall off your ankle like that. And maybe your hand aches when you write? You crack your bones or feel like pulling your fingers? I meant to tell Imogen about it, actually, so she knows that it wasn't...' Zach frowns and looks away from me. 'So that she knows it wasn't caused by anything else.'

He has a lump in his neck that bobs when he swallows. I want to press it into his throat so he shuts up. It's none of his business. I don't like him talking about me and Mam as if he knows us. My ligaments hold me up just fine. He's trying to make us feel weak and floppy so he can be in charge but I won't let him. I should leave but I want to figure out what his plan is. That's what the song was telling me – Zach wants to trap Mam and I have to stop him. He thinks he loves her. Maybe she thinks she loves him? But it's a trick. Only me and Mam truly love each other. We don't need anybody else. There can only be one *best*.

'What was the music you had on before with the man saying a poem? Some of it was French. I know about French words. Mainly starting with A and B but I know some others too.'

Zach does a kind of squint like Mam does when she's trying to read the back of the packet of seeds to see what she's supposed to do. He doesn't know what to do with me.

'You mean the rap?' He ruffles the back of his hair. I bet he doesn't even know all the things his body tells me. I'd beat him at cards no problem. 'Yes, some of it is French hip-hop. I got into it when I lived there for a while. I thought we might move there one day. Anyway, Imogen's on her way.'

That's his plan. He wants to drive away and take Mam to France. He wants to steal her away from me and Halham to have her all to himself. The poison inside is changing her. She isn't herself. What if she agrees and leaves me behind?

The insects awaken. They're so mad. Hordes of them run into my arms and legs. My whole body strengthens. They take over my torso and gather under my tongue. *Shhh* I tell them. 'I'm Mam's best friend.' I whisper. I clench my teeth tight so the creatures can't move my tongue into a different shape to say terrible things.

Zach looks down at my ankle. His wolf-face tries to morph into a worried sheep but I know what he really is. 'Of course, you love your mum very much. But it's good to have friends your own age, too.'

He thinks he's won because him and Mam are the same age but Mam says blood is thicker than water and I know that now. It's thick and strong and full of metal. Me and Mam have the same blood and DNA. It doesn't matter if Mam knew Zach a long time ago, he's an Outsider now.

'Actually, I know how old I am. Mam told me today – I'm thirteen years old which is called a teenager and something about storms in German but it doesn't have to be stormy because Halham is the safest place and we have each other. And I have a friend who is probably the same age. Her name is Alana and we have a special connection because everything is connected in the end – you just have to work out how. Even the daisies know that.'

I'm triumphant. He can hardly keep the shock from his face that I know more than he expected. That feels good. As his power drains, it transfers into me. I reckon he's on twenty per cent battery now which means I'm on eighty per cent. Basic maths. He can't keep the barrier up in his eyes any longer which means I can peek into his mind. He's thinking *Do you know how I'm connected to you?* That's a pointless question because I don't care. I'm going to make him go far away – back to the United States of America.

He says, 'Would you like to see some old photos? I dug some out of Imogen from when she wasn't much older than you are now.'

That's a sneaky move because I want to see those photos so much. I might have underestimated his power levels. He could have been snooping into my mind to read my list of Most Wanted Things which includes old photographs of Mam.

There's no sign of her yet but maybe that's a good thing. She wouldn't want me to see old pictures because she says it's best to live in the here and now. Although lately she's been spending more and more time *not* here.

'Can I see all the ones you have of Mam?' I also want to see pictures of Texas and France but I don't want Zach to think it's him that I'm interested in. It's places. Other places that are far from here.

'They're in the van. Come in and we can get your leg up to rest while you look through. Imogen will be over soon.' I follow Zach around the side of the van to the door. He asks me a question without looking at me. 'You've been in a vehicle before?'

'Yes, I had a ride in Farmer Grove's tractor a while ago.' I'd hated the vibrations that ran through my body as I squeezed in next to Mam. It was supposed to be for fun but I closed my eyes and did my eight times tables which are the hardest of all except for twelves. 'You don't need to put the engine on.'

Inside the van is like a small room. There's a chair that flips down opposite a bench. They're so close together that knees might touch. Tiny purple curtains hang at the sides of the windows. I can't tell if the inside is made of real light-coloured wood or if it's plastic that's pretending. It's good to be able to see familiar trees and skyline through the windows but there's not enough air for two people.

'Can you leave the door open, please.' If Zach squeezes himself in between the front seats, he could start the engine and zoom off with me stuck in the back. *He won't leave without Mam. She's on her way.*

There's a small square table between us. I press my legs back as far as possible to keep us separate. Zach takes out a box with a design of an old map on it. There are multicoloured envelopes filled with photographs. White stickers on the outside of each state the year they were taken. My skin tingles.

'Here's the year we met.' He selects a yellow envelope. I've never seen what Mam looked like before she was a grown-up. Zach tries to take some power percentage back from me by holding the pictures in his hand so he sees them first.

He passes me one. Mam's face is the same but a bit rounder. Her skin is smooth. I'm shocked at how short her hair is compared to our long hair now. She's leaning against a stone wall wearing jeans that nearly cover her boots and a black leather jacket that's too short. I bring the photo up closer to my face, wishing that made it three-dimensional like the headset does. I'd like to climb into that picture and sit with young Mam. She looks happy. I can tell that's her real smile. She's genuinely pleased to be looking at the person holding the camera.

In the next photograph, Mam is at a table with fancy food in front of her. She has glittery eye make-up on and is holding a present wrapped with ribbon. This must be her birthday. Behind her are other people at tables. It's strange to see her outside of Halham, surrounded by strangers as if that doesn't matter at all.

Zach hands me another photograph that shows Mam sitting with her legs crossed on a sandy beach. Her arm reaches up as she holds the camera herself. Zach is next to her. They rest their faces against each other like their cheeks are kissing. His arm is around her. Mam is laughing. She doesn't look worried, or in pain, or pale from bleeding. They belonged to each other long before I was born. Even worse, they could touch.

This confirms my dark, scratching fear: it's me that's the problem.

'It might feel a bit strange looking at these if you've never seen any before. But do you see how similar you are to your mum? And this one has her father in, too.'

Mam stands outside with my grandfather. Her arms are folded and she's doing a tight smile with no teeth on show. I'm surprised to see that his hair, moustache and beard are totally white, as if Father Christmas had stopped being jolly. They stand on either side of a front door. That door slams open into my stomach.

'I know this door.'

Zach turns the photograph towards him and I want to snatch it back even though it's hard to look at. It wasn't long ago that I pulled it tight after my sleepover, happy to leave the holiday house ready for new guests.

'Imogen told me she rents it out now, their old house. That was where they lived back when I used to visit. There was a barn where your house is. The rest looks pretty much the same. Now don't get me wrong – it's a fantastic place to grow up in with such a lot of space but there's a whole world out there. I think it's important that you both get to see some of it one day. Home will always be waiting for you.'

I knew it! Zach wants to get Mam out of Halham. It sounds like he wants to make me leave, too. He doesn't understand that we don't need all those other places.

Even though the door is open, fresh air won't come into the van. We've used up nearly all the oxygen so it's getting hard to breathe. I want to ask Zach all the questions on my list but I can't stay in here any longer. I jump up and run out into the daylight, sucking up as much oxygen as I can to send into my red blood cells. They take it around my whole body, feeding it with energy. My heart is working extra fast to deliver it. I have my strength back that Zach tried to sap by encasing me in his van.

Zach has followed me out and I wish I'd thought to slam the door behind me and barricade it with a plank of wood from the pile at the side of the road. He would be shouting and rattling the door but I'd walk home. On my way, I'd meet Mam and tell her that Zach has decided to leave. We'd have an early supper in the kitchen, eating the cupcakes while they were still warm, back to the two of us.

'I didn't mean to panic you, Cate. I'm sorry if I'm moving too fast. I just want to help you. You deserve a better life than this. I should have come for you both a long time ago. I would have if I'd only known.'

A better life than our perfect life? You can't get better than perfect. It doesn't make any sense. He's come to take us away.

Mam had been keeping us safe from him. She pretended I didn't exist but then he found out. Now she's under his spell, it's down to me to take action. Nobody will ever separate me from Mam or Halham.

I stare at Zach so hard that the rest of my vision goes blurry. I let the creatures run into place down my limbs. They're black, scuttling beetles now with metallic wings for strength. They scurry up into my arms, giving me extra strength.

Before I realise what comes next, they hurl themselves against each thigh in turn to make me run forwards. A swathe of them fills my biceps. There's nothing I can do to stop them. My body belongs to them. It pulsates to the beat of one million spiked legs as my fists smash onto Zach's head so he falls backwards and hits his head against the van, the shock on his face from the power and danger of my touch.

24

IMOGEN

NOW

Imogen closes the door of The Blacksmith's Cottage and leans against it for a short while, needing some respite before transferring herself from present to past. Cate appeared to have managed well with finding out about Zach but there's a risk that everything could move too quickly if she doesn't step back and think. There's so much to consider that her mind teeters on the edge of shutting down. She can't allow that to happen.

Deliberately bypassing the living room at the back of the house, Imogen takes the steep stairs up to where she'd found the evidence when she was only fifteen. There wasn't much left now but she'd felt unable to destroy it, as if that would be another act of self-destruction. The back bedroom reeks of damp. Faded wallpaper in salmon and sage peels away from the edges. Dark patches are wet to the touch. Yellowed nets dangle onto insect corpses. Dust slopes up the corners of the windowsill and covers all surfaces that don't house storage boxes. She can almost taste it: the skin, carpet, hair and soot that has gathered in remembrance. *Dust to dust, ashes to ashes.*

Father wasn't the one who had caught Imogen up here,

wide-eyed and shaking. Perhaps things would have been different if it had been; fewer secrets, less tragedy. No, it had been Toria. What did she used to call her when she was little? The vanilla nurse. Over time, Toria's role had expanded. Imogen had guessed correctly that The Blacksmith's Cottage was where Father hid their affair. But until her discovery in this room, she hadn't realised the extent of Toria's involvement in how the Rounds skewed from visits to a dark business.

On average, they did six sets of the Rounds each week. Sometimes the drive was so long that afterwards they'd sleep in the car before travelling back home. When there wasn't time for classes in the house, Father would teach and test her as he drove. It took years for him to fulfil his promise of finding a way for Imogen to reduce the number of Rounds she was obliged to complete in person. She wonders how much planning from Toria went into making the idea appear spontaneous.

During the two years that Imogen crammed to learn for her GCSEs in between the Rounds and bouts of fitful sleep, Toria had been spending more time at their house.

Her visits had started off as work meetings with schedules laid out on the dining table that Imogen and Father never ate at. Over the years, the piles of paper reduced. Coffee was replaced by wine. Once a week or so, Toria was still downstairs with Father when Imogen went to bed.

They were an unconventional match. Toria was younger and a little eccentric in her style. She favoured handmade earrings from craft fairs in the shape of animals, musical notes or medical equipment.

There was a lightness to her; an ability to let go and enjoy things. Her flawless foundation, eyeliner and pouting pink lips were ever-present, as if she slept that way just in case the fire brigade was called in the early hours.

Father's conservative tastes in all other matters hadn't

stopped the inevitable. Imogen kept herself awake chanting facts or reading books until the front door clicked. Toria never stayed the night and in her small way, Imogen felt that she won each time she heard the front door latch being pulled across.

It wasn't always easy to maintain a dislike of Toria. She was far more playful than Imogen's mother had ever been and seemed to find the most mundane things hilarious or awe-inspiring. Her voice had been warm and hinted at mischief.

'Just look how thick and perfectly straight your hair is, Imogen. You could do any style you like with that and turn every head in the north of England.'

Even though Imogen's greatest desire at that age was to have time to herself with no attention from strangers whatsoever, it felt good to gain Toria's praise. Perhaps she would try a little make-up one day, just for herself.

'I don't really know how to do anything with my hair. I tried to plait it but my fingers kept getting it wrong.' She didn't mention the throbbing, red knuckles that shouted at her to crack them again and again. The Rounds continued to take their toll on her physically.

'Why don't you let me have a go? I could cut it into an amazing sharp bob like that actress – the one who won the award and wore the dress off one shoulder, who goes out with that rapper.'

Imogen had no idea who Toria was talking about but she liked the sound of a *sharp* haircut. That would go well with eyeliner and maybe even a tattoo if she could find a way to get one without Father knowing. Toria could become an ally. Not that Father was the enemy exactly but Imogen noticed that she no longer sought him out once they were home from the Rounds. She crawled under her duvet or sat on the windowsill, wondering what it would be like to camp in the woods.

'If you like.' Imogen shrugged and stopped herself from

checking with Father. She didn't need permission or approval. She decided that it was her hair and so her choice.

But what happened afterwards wasn't her choice; she'd never been given the chance to choose and that's what had hit so hard when she discovered what was in this room in The Blacksmith's Cottage.

Toria had sprayed her hair with water and used kitchen scissors but somehow managed to do an excellent job. The change from long, straggly locks to a sleek bob made Imogen feel almost pretty. She ran to the bathroom to inspect it from every angle. She never questioned what happened to the hair that was left behind or pieced that together with Toria's interest in her health.

Imogen's phone pings with a message. It's so rare for her to receive one that at first she's confused about where the sounds come from, looking around the room at all the packed boxes. The mobile in her bag vibrates again.

It's Zach. *Cate is at the van looking for you.* Followed by *Can you come now?*

Perhaps she should run straight over to maintain control of who knows what, but it feels too late for that. She's in a slow-motion landslide and no amount of scrabbling about to rescue individual rocks will stop it. *Be over shortly* she replies.

There are still some of the little cardboard boxes piled up in the corner. She knows they're mostly empty now. The wares are long gone. The day that Toria found her, there were dozens of the boxes – each filled with around one centimetre length of Imogen's hair. She removed one lid after another, laying her finger on the soft, brown hair that several weeks before had been resting on her shoulders.

It had been a shock when she'd confronted Toria back then.

'What the hell are you doing with this? It's mine!' It was a ridiculous thing to say because Imogen had no intention of taking the hair back. She wanted to burn the whole lot.

'We were hoping to find the right way to explain.' Toria's voice remained smooth. The use of *we* to ostracise Imogen hurt as much as the betrayal of a seemingly innocuous haircut. 'You know I was simply helping your father, who's always trying to do the right thing. You were getting fed up with all the travelling and visits, so he agreed that this might be a way to reduce the demands on you.'

'You send these out instead of me visiting? My dead hair is the same as hours of effort, and concentration, and taking all their pain and contamination into me so I feel broken afterwards. You're saying just my hair could have done that all along? And you didn't tell me?' Imogen felt heat engulf her. She pushed the boxes out of view. They disgusted her. This was a sly fox move, a manipulation of her father and the family's ways.

'You know how much the Rounds means to your father but I helped him see there could be another way. It's like a trial, an experiment, the same as researchers do for new medications. We're collecting the results to check how well it works.'

Imogen had gripped the table. 'Where have you sent them? The care homes? Are you charging for pieces of me?'

Toria momentarily lost her carefully placed composure. Her neck flushed pink. I recalled her Gucci handbag, new leather boots, twinkling gems on her rings.

'This is a very precious gift from you to people in need. We do charge a fee and that's what pays for Halham to continue to run and means I can help out more. It's a burden for your father to keep the buildings and farm running when he's had no time for other work or for our relationship. He's dedicated his entire life to you and helping others.'

It was a burden for Father. *She* was a burden. Nothing more than skin, hair and blood now he'd let Toria's claws into him.

'What's in the other boxes?' She already knows but needs to hear it. Longer boxes lie on the next table with a roll of cotton wool. 'What else have you been selling?'

'There's no need to get upset. Just think how much more good you can do, and with hardly any effort at all.'

Yes, no effort at all apart from her own body replenishing its blood supply only for it to be stolen and sold.

'You said those blood tests were for me. That you wanted to check I wasn't anaemic or whatever. You're a bloody *nurse!* You should be struck off!' Imogen wanted to roar but found her voice shaky as tears poured out, extinguishing her rage. She felt nauseous at the thought of her blood being sold as medicine. Did people drink it? Smear it on their suffering bodies? Inject it into their veins? Imogen crumpled onto the floor. She didn't want to know. She wanted to walk backwards and undo the last hour of her life.

Toria knelt beside her. 'I know it's difficult for you, especially now you're getting older. Your father loves you so much. He knows the good inside you and wants to share it but he shouldn't have to traipse all over the place. It's wearing him out. Only three more years, then you can do whatever you please. There'll be money for you to start a new life – it was never about the money, of course, but that will be your freedom. Please don't ruin this.'

Toria made it sound like a choice. Imogen wasn't sure there really had been one but at the time it suited her to believe it. So, she made a choice to permit their dark trade to continue with the hair and blood already taken on one condition: Toria had to end her relationship with Father and be an absent business partner. If Toria really loved him she'd choose love over money. Imogen never saw her at Halham again and Father aged a decade over a few weeks at her absence.

Imogen served her time. Father's money transferred to her

bank account on her eighteenth birthday and allowed her to build a home and life for Cate.

Imogen will not return to a life that is dictated by the beliefs of a man she loves. If Zach doesn't understand, she will do what she has to. The ends justify the means.

25

CATE

Time disappears altogether until Mam arrives. I hear her call my name before I see her. My hand throbs.

'Cate, where are you?'

Zach is sitting on the ground, leaning against the van with his hand on the back of his head. I wish I could rewind time. I'd start all over again as a baby when it's just me and Mam with no worries. We'd do it differently this time. I wouldn't ask so many questions. I'd be the best girl. No need to visit the holiday house or sit in the farmer's field. We'd be happy together.

'Oh, there you both are. Zach, what happened? Are you okay?'

Zach gets to his feet, a little unsteady. He avoids looking at me. No wonder. Bad girl causing bad things. 'Why don't we go back to the house where there's room to sit and we can have a drink and chat.'

Mam doesn't know what happened. I'm so relieved I could throw up. But it also means we are further away from each other than ever.

I'm panting as if I've run around the whole field. I try to slow my breath back down to normal to cover up what happened. Mam is in one of her moods where things are already decided. She's the director now. I'm glad. I seem to make a mess of things if I try to solve problems myself. I should have trusted her. Mam's walking faster than usual so we trail behind her. I don't turn around. Zach will be out of here by the end of the day. Mam's fast legs and voice means she is in charge now, even if it's a difficult thing to do. This is the way she cleaned out the bloody coop when the chickens were killed and how she organised Farmer Grove to collect the ones who survived. I need to copy that strong, clear voice that doesn't have any wobble in it. What's the point of feelings when they get in the way of what you need to do?

Zach jogs ahead to catch up with Mam. He knows I can't go fast with my ankle so he's getting his own back on me for hurting him. What if he tells her all about it? I can't make out what they're saying but Zach is doing most of the talking and Mam is still stomping ahead. He doesn't know her moods like I do.

Mam stops and whirls around. 'Change of plan. Zach and I have some things to discuss. Why don't you go and play for a while then join us later for tea?'

The cakes! I put the oven on, but never put the cupcakes in to cook like I promised. 'I need to do my baking. I'll stay in the kitchen to do it.' I was going to add that I won't eavesdrop but the truth is I will. I need to.

'There's plenty of time for that. They won't take long. Now, why don't you go to the playground for a while? We can do the afternoon tea later like we planned.'

I hang my head down. I want to act as normal as possible but if I'm not in the house, I don't get to check what Zach says or to show Mam that I'm on her side. 'I think I'll look the seedlings over.' It's better to stay close. I won't let Zach push me out or fill Mam's ears with more poison.

He says, 'Imogen, look at her ankle. She should be resting not running off to play or doing gardening. That's what I'm trying to explain, about hypermobility syndrome.'

Mam holds her hand up to stop Zach talking. I turn slightly so she can't see my ankle but she doesn't try to. If she was a colour, it would be silver. She's solid metal now. He's failed to soften her. Mam is back to how she should be. I want to stay with her but it's more important that I show I'm on Mam's side. The pain doesn't matter at all, it's just a sensation like being itchy or hot.

'Let's get back to the house, Zach. Cate's doing fine. She knows how to take care of herself in Halham and the fresh air will do her good. There's no work to be done today. The playground is the best place for her.'

I've been given my instructions. So has Zach.

'Okay, I'll go for a little while then come home.'

'Good girl, I'll see you later.'

That proves it – I'm a good girl. Halham will heal me. I'll take the long route around the village and make sure everything is the way it should be before we get rid of Zach. He doesn't belong here.

It's important to do things in the right order. I need to figure out what that is, but it's hard to think clearly. I try to put all my most important places into alphabetical order but the pictures in my head get interrupted. Climbing frame, corner shop, farmer's field, gates, (head bashed against metal), hedgerows, holiday house, (swish of my fist flying through the air, thwack of it against his skull), vegetable patch, view of Hart Hill.

I ignore the path and walk diagonally across the playground to get to our field without going near to the house. My legs feel funny, as if my feet are too far away to control. I pick a dandelion and rest my palm on the fuzz to make my fingers pay attention.

The jackdaws squawk and squabble above me. Two swoop down on a third in attack. It drops and for a moment I'm scared that it's going to crash to the ground but it changes direction into the tallest tree in Halham. Branches shake as the birds battle. The caws overlap, black shapes shifting behind greenery. Then, the silence of a truce that can't be trusted.

I arrive at the field with my ears still echoing with the jackdaws' shrieks. Everything looks just as it should. Zach's poison is no match for nature. Green covers the land from my feet to the horizon in this direction. Grass, hedgerows, out further to the woods. It looks like it's green to the end of the world. But I know the Earth is a sphere. I like the way that word *sphere* feels in my mouth. It's got *here* in it, too. Wherever you are, that's the top of the world. You can't ever fall off. The Earth keeps you safe on its surface by pulling you close with a force called gravity, which doesn't ever switch off or run out. Some days, gravity pulls extra hard, like when Mam couldn't get out of bed. Other days, it loosens its hold a little so you can float.

I lie down on my side and press my ear to the ground. There's a very distant rumble. I can feel it in vibrations as much as I can hear it. My entire body is listening to what lies below. I curl my knees up to my chest as tight as I can. I don't want to listen to any thoughts that try to guess what Mam is saying to Zach, how close they stand to each other, what Mam's face will change to if Zach tells her about what I did. I only want to be as close as possible to the centre of the Earth, where the pull to the core is irresistible.

'This time, only one hand!'

I peek up. It's Alana! She does a cartwheel with one arm tucked into her, then whoops as she takes a bow. There's nobody else around.

I jump up and clap. 'That was amazing!'

Alana beams at me and hurls her small body into another

somersault. She's good at letting go of gravity. Maybe we are opposites; north and south poles, pulled together. She waves then does a kind of double flip. Her body is the opposite of mine too: extra bendy and graceful compared to my stiff, clunky arms and legs. Even her fingers are beautiful as she points her arms into the air. I pull at my index finger behind my back until it clicks. Alana runs over to me and puts her palm up to face me. I'm unsure what to do, so copy her. Then she taps my hand with hers and giggles. It's the briefest of touches. I don't feel panic. I don't feel crushed or cross or frightened. That's because we are attracted instead of repulsed. It's okay, I'm sure of it.

'I was hoping to see you. I've been so bored. My mum brought loads of work to do and Dad keeps staring at his kindle. He says I shouldn't need the telly or even the iPad because it's good to have a break from them. He won't even give me the wifi code. So mean.'

She huffs and I want her to be huffing at her parents not me, so I don't say that I have no idea what she's talking about. It doesn't matter. We are real friends because she is telling me a secret. I need to make myself interesting, too.

'I found out that the house you're staying in is Mam's old house. She lived there with her father a long time ago. He died suddenly but she won't tell me much about him or what happened.'

Alana's eyes open wide. I feel a horrible squeeze around my stomach in case I've said the wrong thing.

'Did he die in the house I'm staying at? Do you think that's why she won't talk about it? If it was a long time ago, he wasn't that old when he died.' She leans closer to me. 'Maybe something happened, and now he's a ghost, haunting the house because he can't be at peace?'

'Are ghosts fact or fiction, or in between?'

Alana is smaller than me but she seems more like a grown-up. I can see now why her father talked to me in that strange way, as if I was much younger than her.

'Oh, one hundred per cent fact. I've been listening to a podcast called *Ghostly Britain*. They can even measure how much of a presence there is in a building. This machine goes off the scale in some rooms, there's no faking that. It's not scary, though. Little kids and stupid films have got it all wrong. It's just about communication. Do you know what I mean?'

I don't know about ghosts, or pods, or machines. But I do know about secret communication. It would be easier to explain if the blackbird was here but there's no sign of him. He may be hiding after the kerfuffle with the jackdaws.

'I think so.' My tongue isn't sure if I should tell her. It sticks to the roof of my mouth, undecided. Then a gust of wind crosses the field and ripples the grass. 'See how the grass just bowed towards us, one blade at a time? It's so fast that it looks like the whole field is waving. The grass communicates.'

Alana looks out to the field then back at me. 'Yep. And did you know that mushrooms send electrical signals to each other and that's kind of like their language? That was on the news so it's true. Dad was totally overexcited about it. I wonder what they say to each other?'

I got it right and my friend didn't laugh at me. I want to cry but in a happy way. I don't in case I can't switch it off and I flood the whole field with my salty tears and nothing can ever grow again. Maybe I'm interesting after all. My friend believes me. She's choosing to spend time with me.

'And birds too! They know a lot because they can find out so much from up high with their extra good eyes and ears. If you listen carefully, they can tell you things.'

Alana does a very slow nod with her lips together like she's thinking hard. 'You're totally right and guess what, some birds are psychopomps. I learnt that from Stephen King. It means they communicate with the dead. So, if you're good at understanding birds, they could tell you what your grandfather wants to say, and that could be what needs to happen to stop him being a ghost. Then he can rest in peace.'

And just like that, the lines that connect me and Alana come together to something important. This has turned from the worst to the best day of my life.

'Let's go to the swings!' I want to make the most of the day and have more scenes of me and my friend to put in my top memories list. We wander over to the playground. I let Alana have the tyre swing which is the best one. We spend time kicking our legs forwards and backwards as fast as we can, then we lift our legs to let gravity do the work for us.

'What else is there to do around here? We could go round the shops or see what's on at the cinema? It's too quiet here. Dad says I should enjoy my own company, but why be selfish? I should let lots of other people enjoy my company.'

Alana laughs so I laugh along with her. She must go to lots of different places outside of her home and the holiday house. I try to make my swing move at the same rate but can't quite match hers. I don't want the afternoon to end. Mam and Zach are in my house right now. The yucky feeling comes up from the back of my throat when I think about it. How can I keep Alana talking when I can't answer her questions? I want to tell her that I've never left Halham but then she might realise I've got nothing to talk about.

'I don't go to many places. How about we play a game instead? We could do hide and seek or alphabet game or a treasure hunt?'

Alana drags her bright white trainers on the ground to stop the tyre moving. 'Is that what you play with your friends?'

I keep swinging. Up, down, up, down. 'It's what I play with

Mam but we don't have to do any of that. We can do whatever you want. You could teach me your games?'

I'm getting it wrong. *I'm* wrong.

Alana jumps off the swing then stands in front of me and grabs the chains so that I stop, too. She's already in charge. That's better because I have no idea what to do or say, and now the bad feelings are trying to push up from where I'd squashed them.

'It's a bit weird here,' she says. 'There aren't the normal things to do. Don't you get bored?'

I think of my top ten places, games, lessons, plants, memories. There's a lot to do. It's nice to know exactly what something is going to be like before you do it – that way there are no scary surprises. But I guess there aren't any nice surprises, either. Or there weren't until Alana arrived.

'It's not boring with you!'

Alana grins and it turns me golden on the inside. 'I can teach you some games that your Mam doesn't play with you. I know all the best ones. I've figured out what we should do.'

Alana talks as if she knows everything for a fact. She's so certain. I don't know how to be normal. Could my friend teach me to be more like her?

'Okay, I can learn fast if you tell me the rules.'

'Let's play truth or dare. I choose Truth. So you ask me a question, a really hard one, and I will tell you the truth.'

I don't know any hard questions. Maybe about maths or geology? Then I realise this could be my chance to ask a question from my list. Alana can't answer about Mam or my grandfather but she does know about the Outside. 'What's outside of Halham? I mean, what did you see when you were in the car, before you got here?'

Alana slides her legs open so far that her whole body drops to the floor with one leg in front of her and one behind. It looks a bit like her legs have been chopped off. She doesn't seem to be in pain. 'I'll answer but you have to go first. I'll ask you a Truth question. Do you go to school or away on holiday or to the shopping centre?'

I grip harder onto the chains so I don't fall off. Alana tips her head to the side like my blackbird.

'No.'

She rolls onto her side then jumps up. 'I knew it! Is it because you're not allowed? Like, are you not well or something? I heard this podcast about a boy that was allergic to the twenty-first century. He got a rash and couldn't breathe if he went near anything modern because his body couldn't handle the chemicals. I think he had to live in a plastic bubble and his parents had to wear these spacesuits to even touch him.'

'I don't know. I'm not supposed to touch anyone. Mam hasn't exactly said I'm not allowed to leave, I just never do because it's safe here.'

Alana sits cross-legged on the grass. I get off the swing to sit opposite her. 'That's extra. Outside of here is not much really: countryside and a tiny village with a shop and one pub. But it's not that far to town and I saw signs for Chester on the way here which is a really old place with black and white buildings where they film *Hollyoaks*. You know, from TV?'

I don't answer.

'There's a massive shopping village that has all these discounted stores that's pretty good. You should ask your mum to take you to get some new clothes.'

I look down at my blue trousers and white T-shirt which Mam embroidered with a bunch of lavender onto the pocket because it's my favourite flower.

'We've done Truth so next is Dare. I dare you to leave. Not forever, I mean let's just get out of here, me and you. My dad doesn't want me to play with you, but I don't care. We could go tonight while he's watching the match. Eight o'clock?'

No, no, no. But I don't want to lose my first friend. This might be what thirteen-year-olds do. It's just a game, nothing bad. Probably.

'How?' Even asking the question crosses a line, as much as reaching my hand out of Halham.

'I'll meet you here. Pretend you're going to bed early then sneak out. You'll figure it out. I'll pack us some snacks and bring my pocket money. Wear a coat with a hood.'

My head nods along but I'm already separated from it. I'm floating; watching a girl and her friend make plans that could change the entire world.

26

IMOGEN

AGE 7

Imogen hadn't wanted to go in the car with her mother who didn't sing songs or know jokes like Father. She was always pressuring Imogen to do awful things like join the Brownies or go to a local primary school.

The waiting room was painted with Disney characters that didn't look quite right. Snow White, who should be in a forest, was next to The Little Mermaid, who should be in water. Cinderella was too old. Peter Pan was cross. Posters showed smiling parents with a hand on their child's shoulder. Imogen hoped that nobody expected her mother to smile that way while looking at her – she was much better at huffing out a sigh.

'You must answer all the lady's questions politely. She'll know if what you say is the truth or a lie, that's her job.'

Imogen didn't like the sound of this lady who was a lie-catcher. Why did Father say she had to come here without him? At least he'd rolled his eyes at her mother which meant they were still on the same team. One night, Imogen had heard her mother screech that she'd pack her bags and leave if things didn't change. After she banged her bedroom door shut, Imogen had crept downstairs and sat on Father's lap. Neither of them mentioned what had been said. They didn't need to. All they had to do was wait. Then it would just be the two of them forever.

A lady arrived. 'Imogen? Why don't you come with me?'

The lady was short and flowery. She had a multicoloured scarf wrapped around her neck even though she was indoors. She floated down to a room that had 'Do Not Disturb' written on paper and blu-tacked to the door. Inside, there were bean bags, boxes of toys, a doll's house, a table with pens and paper and a red sofa. It was much better than the waiting room. There was a black camera in the top corner of the room which pointed down at the play area. Imogen's mother remained in the doorway and pushed her inside.

The lady swiped her hand in invitation to be seated. 'Actually, I usually meet with both the parent and child for my assessment.'

'That won't be necessary. You'll find out what you need from Imogen. There's nothing wrong with me, and her father refused to come, so that's that.'

Imogen knew when her mother said "that's that" it meant there was no point saying please, slamming a door, or giving sensible five-point reasons for disagreeing. She didn't need her mother there, anyway. It would only spoil the fun. Imogen chose a yellow cushion, slipped off her shoes and waited. The pens were big-girl ones that couldn't be rubbed out. There was a Sindy doll propped outside the doll's house like a giant. She had red curly hair and a tracksuit. Pipe cleaners poked like giant spider legs out of a drawer that said *art supplies*. Imogen wasn't afraid.

'I suppose we can continue without you present, if Imogen is willing to? I must insist that you stay in the waiting room should she need you or become upset.'

Imogen's mother snorted. 'Oh, she doesn't need a mother

apparently, only her beloved father who can do no wrong! You see what you make of it all, in your professional opinion!' She jabs the air to make the dots that go on the bottom of each exclamation mark. 'Get to the bottom of what they do on their trips! That girl should be in school!'

Imogen thought it was a shame the video camera didn't move to whoever was talking like it did for television programmes. If Father could watch a recording of it, he would roll his eyes so hard, they'd get stuck and Imogen would have to tap the back of his head to knock them back the right way.

The lady closed her office door and sat in a leather chair. Imogen was itching to pick up the Sindy doll or use the red felt tip but she knew there were questions first. The day before, Father had explained to her the rules of answering. It wasn't hard at all. Not for her clever brain.

'My name is Jessica. Your mother has asked me to meet you today and see how things are. My job is to help children who may have tricky things inside like worries or feeling cross or sad.'

The tricky things were mostly outside but Imogen knew she mustn't interrupt.

'I'd like to get to know about you and I have lots of toys and craft items to use. Is that okay?'

Rule one – show you are happy and fine. Imogen nodded and showed Jessica her best smile. 'I feel happy today and also I feel fine.'

Jessica smiled back but then jotted something in her notebook.

'Your mummy said you don't go to school for your learning?'

Rule two – show you are clever. 'I do my lessons with Father. We cover the correct curriculum. I like reading and comprehension the most.' Imogen was pleased that she'd practised the four syllables of curriculum and delivered them flawlessly.

'Great, and what does comprehension mean, Imogen?' Jessica held her pen in the air, ready to write down the answer. Father explained it all. She wasn't asking because she didn't know the answer, even though that's what Imogen's mother did sometimes. She was asking to try to catch Imogen out and make Father look like he wasn't doing a good job. Wouldn't her mother be thrilled with that!

'It means that you understood what you were reading.'

'Okay, good. So, you like learning and I can see that you're clever.' Imogen puts a tick in her mind next to rule numbers one and two. 'What about how you get along with other people? Home schooling can be great but it can also be hard not to be with children your own age. I know you don't have any brothers or sisters.'

The lady said that as if it was a sad thing, instead of the best thing in the world. Imogen knew other people wouldn't understand that she only needed Father – other children were too little and dull for her. She had prepared this answer which was mostly a lie but Father said it's called a white lie when it's for a good reason and wasn't bad at all.

'I play with my cousins, and sometimes we do shared lessons with Bethany and Bridgit from next door.' *Rule two-and-a-half, added by Imogen – don't mention that Bethany and Bridgit are knitted toads that you were given by a crinkly old woman in a nursing home.* 'We do fun games and also plant fruit and vegetables for old people.'

'Thank you for explaining that to me. Now, one more question before we play. I've just met your mummy. Can you describe your daddy to me?'

This was the one Imogen had to be very careful about. The lie-catcher was looking for clues. *Third rule – don't let anybody know about the Rounds or your special gift. Move them on to talk about your mother.*

'Father is six foot tall. He likes to read and learn. He smells like a spray called Desert Heat. His favourite food is spaghetti. He's nicer than my mother because he never gets cross or tells me to shut up or that I ruined his life.' Imogen's mother had never said she ruined her life, but her face and sighs said it, so that was kind of telling the truth.

Jessica made a note then leant back in her chair. Her eyes had become a little narrower which was a good thing – she'd noticed the horrible things that Imogen's mother said and didn't like that one bit.

'It sounds like things can be a little bit difficult at home sometimes. Tell me about what happens when you're out of the house?'

Imogen was glad that Father taught her what to look out for. Her mouth was so fast at replying sometimes that she could have got it wrong if she hadn't known to be careful.

'You said we would play and do art after the last question.' *Fourth and final rule – stay in control, whatever it takes.* 'Keeping promises is very important.'

Jessica blinked twice then nodded. Her face was hard to read. Imogen made sure her own was freeze-framed on a slight smile.

'You're quite right. I did say that, and I keep my word in this room.'

Her language choice seemed as careful as Imogen's. She kept her word inside of the room but not out of the room? Did she usually break promises and tell fibs all over the shop when she wasn't at work? Imogen would like to catch her out in real life. She could follow her. Jessica would tell the lady on reception, "I'm going to study at the library" but Imogen would find out she went home and dozed on the couch instead. She'd take a photo and send it to the clinic. When Jessica came back to work, her boss would shake his head and say, "You're a liar. I'm afraid you can't have this job. All the children who see you don't have to come anymore." That thought was as satisfying as a chocolate biscuit.

'Here's the doll's house you can use next.'

The doll's house was made of real wood with a roof painted black and white like the oldest buildings Imogen and Father passed on their way to the Rounds. It was grander than their real house but completely empty. All the tiny furniture and figures were piled in boxes.

'Would you like to set it up?'

Imogen wasn't sure if that was a question or instruction but it didn't matter – she'd already decided to do that, so the lie-catcher didn't win. There were two rooms downstairs which should be a kitchen and living room. Imogen lined up a washing machine, sink and cooker along the back wall. She chose a round table with two high-backed chairs to eat at. For the living area, the sofas looked too uncomfortable made from wood.

'Can I use things from that art box?'

Jessica passed the box which was crammed with all sorts of materials. There was a roll of cotton wool that Imogen pulled two clumps of to form two comfortable cloud chairs. On the right-hand side she wedged a bookcase that had lots of fake book spines along each shelf. Movement flashed behind her. Jessica was writing in her notebook again. Imogen froze to assess what she'd done that caught the lie-catcher's attention. The bookcase leant against a painted door. As soon as she placed it there, the scratchy writing started.

'That door isn't real, you can't open it, so it doesn't matter that I've covered it.' Imogen didn't like the feeling of her heart going too fast. The final rule was as slippery as soap while the lady watched her. She hadn't been careful enough.

'There's no right or wrong.'

Imogen felt a little buzz in her belly. She'd figured something out: this lady wasn't the lie-catcher; *she* was. Jessica said there was no wrong way but it wasn't true because she only wrote in her notebook when she didn't like what Imogen did. It could have made her angry or scared but instead it felt good. Father would be impressed at her detective skills.

The two rooms in the top part of the house were still bare. Imogen needed to figure out what to do so that Jessica would tell her mother there was nothing wrong with her. She had to protect Father and the Rounds. The trouble was, she didn't know which items were the right ones. Should she make a bathroom? Or two bedrooms? A playroom to show how she knew the dolls needed to have fun? Or a classroom for the doll's house children to do important learning?

Imogen turned to Jessica and smiled. 'It's all done. The upstairs is closed today.'

Jessica tipped her head to the side. That could be good, bad, or in between. She didn't write anything down so Imogen decided that had gone well.

'Are there any people in this house?'

'Oh yes, I was going to put them in next.' Imogen longed to pick up the Sindy doll but she was clearly way too big for the house. She made sure she didn't look at it so that Jessica wouldn't know and scribble in her book. In the box, there were Lego figures, small wooden dolls in real clothes and Sylvanian Families creatures.

Jessica's pen hovered over the next page. What was she looking for? Imogen's mother said her daughter was weird and that she needed to learn how to be a little girl by spending more time with children and less time with Father. Imogen needed to show the lie-catcher that she could play nicely and normally. At home, pretend play wasn't really what she'd spend her time doing. She didn't need dolls or toys. Her mind could take her anywhere she wanted to go. She also loved word games and quizzes that she and Father played in the car – make the number plate letters into the longest word you can or list the counties of England. But here, she must do what seven-year-olds do who don't have a brilliant father or a brilliant mind.

Imogen rifled through the box, moving the Sylvanian Families characters to a separate pile away from the mismatching characters. A family was supposed to have a mummy, daddy, brother, sister and baby. She knew that from the boxes of toys she'd seen at Christmas in the department store. Imogen picked up a brown bear wearing a checked shirt under dungarees and placed him just inside the house. His feet were chewed, making him wobble. Next, she chose a little bear with a pink skirt and rammed her next to the daddy to stop him falling over. Surely the lie-catcher would write something down if all the characters toppled over.

A white cat in a floral dress was just right to go into the kitchen to make food. There was a little kitten that had no clothes on at all. Imogen wasn't sure if it was a boy or girl baby but didn't think that mattered. She placed the baby at the mummy's feet where it could crawl around but with someone looking after it to keep it safe. Imogen was pleased that she thought of that. She may have lost points if she stuck the baby upstairs all on its own. It was so little and useless by itself and the mummy cat needed some company so she didn't meow *what about me, nobody loves me.*

'Is that everybody that belongs here?'

There needed to be a brother. A sheep boy in a green outfit would do. He belonged outside like all smelly sheep do, out in the fields, where he'd do exactly the same as all the other stupid sheep. He'd probably follow any rules and never do anything exciting. He'd look the same as all the other lambs. Imogen placed him on the ground a little distance from the doll's house. Jessica lifted her pen and Imogen's stomach squeezed tight. What had she done wrong? It was the silly sheep. She snatched him up and threw him back into the box. Nobody needs a boy in their family anyway.

'I changed my mind, I don't need that one. It's all finished now. Can we do some drawing?'

'Can you tell me what happens next in this house?'

Imogen crunched her teeth together so the lady couldn't tell she was cross. *Rule one – be fine and happy.* 'They have a lovely day.'

Jessica came right up to the house as if she was going to mess it all up. 'See here?' She pointed to the washing machine. 'There's a fire that's started. It's going up the walls of the house. Can you show me what happens next?'

No, no, no, there's no fire in the house. What a nasty lady. 'The fire goes out of the window to the outside. No problem. The cats like how warm it is.'

She moved the white cat and its baby out of the doll's house onto a patch of carpet. The baby cried and cried but couldn't be heard from inside the beautiful house. Imogen didn't say that the fire had spread. It fanned out across the carpet and caught the floating material of Jessica's dress. Flames ran up to her earrings, her scarf, all her fluffy hair.

'And the bears, they close the door and decide to hibernate. They're going to stay at home and sleep for a few months. Their tummies are full and they don't need to go outside at all. They're warm and cosy together.' She laid them both down on cotton wool chairs to sleep.

'Thank you for showing me, Imogen. How do you feel now you've reached the end of the story?'

The lie-catcher hadn't written anything else down. She hadn't asked about the Rounds or anything more about what it was like at home. Imogen had won. She stayed in control and her mother had failed. Smoke filled the room. It flew up Jessica's nostrils and smothered the cats while they slept.

'I feel like it's time to go home.'

27

CATE

I don't eavesdrop on purpose. My body is lighter than usual so Mam and Zach don't hear me return home. I'm the Outsider now.

Zach's voice isn't as calm as when he spoke to me outside his van. 'You're not making sense. You've been here so long, living like this as though it's normal, that you can't see it.'

Mam's voice is jagged in reply. Her consonants could cut into him. 'Cate is my number one priority. You're the one who's brainwashed if you can't see that this is the best way to protect her from the kind of life I had. People don't change. The demands out there will be just the same.'

Through the crack of the living-room door, I see Zach pacing up and down. Mam stands firm with her hands on her hips.

'A few visits to places outside of here is nothing like doing the Rounds! Please just think about it. You wouldn't act like your father. She could start to understand the world and learn to do everyday things like buying something for herself in a shop or being around groups of people.'

'Yes, but what could all that lead to? The first time she leans against someone in a queue who has an injury? Or is recognised as my daughter? Tongues would start wagging from town out to all villages about there being another girl at Halham. She'd be accosted in the street, over social media, more people banging on our gates to lay pressure on her.'

Zach places his hands on each of Mam's shoulders. 'Has she ever watched television or used the internet? She's never walked down an ordinary street, eaten ice cream in a café, chatted to a group of kids her own age while out on her bike. She's never seen the sea. You had a difficult time at her age but you still got to do all that stuff. I know you love her and try your hardest to protect her. But please step back and think about what you really want for her.'

Mam pushes his hands away. I'm frozen in my place.

'You don't get it. We still get desperate people rattling the gates some days, a decade is nothing in these parts; stories carry for centuries. Then the pressure would start; the touching, the demands, the false friendships that are only to get her close to a sick relative. You have no idea how quickly her life would stop being her own.' Mam's voice cracks. 'I wouldn't be the one making her use the gift; her own guilt would be enough.'

It's about touch. It's about why I never leave Halham. But I don't understand what she means. I remember all the times there have been people at our gates, shouting to come in. How Mam switched off the buzzer so we could pretend there was nobody there. She said they wanted to get into the village, but maybe they wanted something from us?

'I saw what you went through but honestly, it was your father's delusion. You must know that deep down. You're an adult now, surely you can see it was play-acting?'

'You didn't feel it like I did. Your clever explanation about hypermobility only explains the pain after. But I could feel so much *during* the Rounds; I could feel when it was working, and I sometimes saw people improve right in front of my eyes.'

Zach's voice gets quieter the more they argue, as if Mam is turning the dial down on him. His speech is slow but that won't help the words pierce through to Mam; she has her armour on. 'He was taking advantage of a child's imagination. Those villagers were desperate to believe some magic could cure them, a short-term placebo. It's not your fault, it was all you'd ever known. But please, Imogen, you've got to see there's no risk to Cate because there is nothing to pass on to her. She's just an ordinary girl.'

I wish I was an ordinary girl. A normal, middling, ordinary girl.

I step into the room, unable to stop the ugly truth from spilling out. 'No, I'm not ordinary.'

They both turn to me. I look between them at the wall so I don't lose my nerve. 'I did a terrible thing to you today because being touched by me is dangerous.'

I drop my head down. I can't look at Mam. It's Zach who replies while she stays silent. 'It was a bit of a shove, that's all, love, because you were feeling overwhelmed.'

'I shouldn't have done it. I didn't mean to. The insects under my skin made me extra strong when I hit you, like I couldn't stop it. Just one hit can be dangerous.'

'Imogen, you told her about what happened? Is that why she's so confused with what's past and present?'

Mam's mouth hangs open as she shakes her head slowly. Zach doesn't understand. I'm not confused, I'm confessing.

'No, I'm not confused. The insects got mad about you wanting to take us away from Halham. I hit you to make you go away, so it can be just me and Mam again like it should be. I wanted to make it safe again. But I don't think it is. I don't think I'm somebody safe.'

Nobody speaks or moves. I'm making it even worse. How am I supposed to know what the right thing to do is?

Zach looks like he might cry and I don't know how to feel about it. I want him to leave us alone but he's the only one who can loosen the double knot of the bag where all Mam's secrets have been tied up.

There's no red anger left in me. My bones are soft. If I drop to the floor, would anyone catch me?

Mam looks exhausted. I hate to see her sad. I can tell her mind is busy, her spider's web of thoughts linking all the things that she hasn't told me about her past, all the things she wants to get right for our future. Instead of being the spider in charge of her web, now she's the fly, trapped in sticky lines, unable to untangle from them. She pants from the effort of thrashing about inside her mind.

'Zach, can you please give me and Cate some time together?'

He looks uncertain. 'It's important that we all talk about this.' He looks much younger now his face is warped by worry. We could be siblings.

'Now isn't the time for talking. Cate needs to rest and recover, and that's that.'

I watch him gather his things. He's no longer the laid-back Zach with shoulders that jiggle when he laughs. He's as slow and careful as me and Mam are when we get too close to the edge of a steep truth, trying not to crash on the rocks below.

'I'll go now and sleep in the van. I'll come back in the morning?'

The house creaks with relief as he leaves. I wish again that I could rewind time. I want to be little again and lie next to Mam like we are the only people in the whole wide world.

'Can we go and lie on your bed?'

Mam doesn't answer but she turns so I follow her up the

stairs to her bedroom. We lie next to each other, flat on our backs. A breeze blows through the open window, carrying the melody of my blackbird into the room for comfort. A tractor rattles in the distance. Outside the house, Halham carries on as if nothing has happened. It's trying to reassure me that it will never change.

I feel the need to continue my confession. The only way for me and Mam to get back to closeness is to wash away the lies from my skin and start again.

'I'm sorry but I planned to break the rules. I agreed to meet my friend tonight. She is staying at the holiday house and her name is Alana. She dared me to run away. And also, I didn't tell you when it happened but I know a secret gate out of Halham. I put my hand through it and into the woods when I was cleaning the holiday house, which I know is ours. That's the bad hand. It's the one that hit Zach.'

Mam sighs the sound of the sea. I know because it's the same shhh that you can hear inside a shell that's soaked up the sound and kept it held secret until somebody bothered to listen.

'There's nothing bad about you, do you hear me? You are a sweet, lovely, innocent girl.'

'I won't go to meet her. I'm sorry. I was being stupid and selfish.'

'You are neither of those words. I understand that you're getting to an age where you're curious about the world. All I've ever wanted was to give you the best childhood possible. It's my job to protect you, in a way I never was protected. But please stay at home. You must promise me that you'll never run away.'

It seems ridiculous that I'd even considered being apart from Mam. Sometimes it's what I thought I wanted, but I was wrong. This is where I belong. I stamp this moment into my top three memory list forever; the day we tell the truth.

'I promise.'

'It must be hard for you to make sense of what Zach and I were talking about. I'll try my best to explain. Do you remember the day you wanted to rescue the chick? It was already dead or at least close to it but your kind heart wanted to make it better.'

I can feel the soft moss on my palm, see Mam's horrified face, feel the squeeze of shame in my throat.

'Yes.'

'Well, I never explained myself because I didn't know how to. I overreacted perhaps. I was afraid of what might happen if somehow, that chick started to stir. I was scared of what you'd find out – what we'd both find out. Once you know something, Cate, you can't choose to not know it. After that, even not doing anything with the knowledge becomes a choice. That's always been my dilemma.'

I'm scared but I listen extra hard and don't try to float away in my own water. This is the kind of scared that comes before you do a new thing for the first time, like hanging upside down from the swing.

'I'm going to tell you a story. Then you'll understand. This story is called *The Rounds*. Once upon a time, there was a tiny girl called Immy who lived with her father.'

Our hands lie side by side on the memory foam, almost touching.

28

IMOGEN

AGE 17 AND 364 DAYS

The eve of Imogen's eighteenth birthday arrived at the end of a month filled with disturbed sleep and crushing headaches. Father tried to be jovial all day but couldn't hide his disappointment that she'd failed to carry out her duty of delivering his granddaughter to take her place. Over the years, Imogen realised his love was conditional; a legal document with caveats and clauses.

Although Father always claimed he had no gift himself, was it truly coincidence that Imogen found herself in this predicament as she became an adult – thirteen weeks pregnant, just as instructed? Or was that the power of the gift turned into a curse?

She hadn't told Zach or visited the doctor. Her precise cycle was sufficient. That and her dark, stretched nipples she couldn't stand to see. Her body would soon be alien and there would be no way to cover up the inevitable growth.

It had crossed Imogen's mind not to go through with the pregnancy. Agency had skipped from grandfather to baby with no room for her to forge a life of her own. But once her body started to whisper the truth of what grew inside her, Imogen realised that the foetus was as much a part of her as her lungs and heart. *Fourth and final rule – stay in control, whatever it takes.* She hadn't told Zach yet because then it would no longer be her secret; no longer be something that was only for her.

The day had passed slowly. Even the simplest elements of Imogen's life took on a new quality, steeped in nostalgia and signifying the end of life as she'd known it. The orange tubs that she'd carried snacks in for long journeys on the Rounds lay upside down on the draining board. The wall calendar that logged their upcoming visits had disappeared from the brickwork in the laundry room. Even the uncomfortable old gentleman's chair with its threadbare velvet covering seemed sad today; the place she used to sit on Father's knee when she was small enough to fit perfectly. Imogen couldn't explain why her imminent freedom also felt like a loss. She'd miss the certainty of a structured life.

'You're sure you don't want to head into town? We should be celebrating.' Zach had noticed her spiky mood. The conflation of the end of the Rounds with the start of adulthood had ruined Imogen's birthday as a thing to be celebrated. Every beginning requires an ending.

Zach stroked the back of her hand. It felt like an invasion. Imogen busied herself with decorating a cake. She was doing it for Father not herself, some semblance of normality on this final night of her belonging to him, her final night belonging to Halham. Funds would enter her account in the morning, then she and Zach would take off to the coast. That was the plan they discussed, at least. Imogen had looked into other options. She'd packed her bags not knowing if they were for a trip with her boyfriend or the start of a new life alone. No, not alone; with her baby. With luck, it would be a boy. But somehow, she already knew that it was a girl. There was no fighting fate.

'I haven't told Father that we're leaving. I want to give him tonight. He's going to take the cake, some drinks and nibbles over to The Blacksmith's Cottage. I think he's actually decorated it, as if I'm still five years old, ready to sing in my birthday at midnight.'

Zach stood behind Imogen and wrapped his arms around her waist. A few months ago, she would have leaned back on him, appreciating his solidity. Now, it caused her to stiffen, as if he might reach through her skin, into her womb to take the baby for himself.

'We're going to Wales, not New Zealand. Not yet, anyway.'

Imogen envied his wanderlust. She wanted to be as excited as him about the possibilities, all those places around the world waiting for them. He wanted to experience them in real life whereas she was happy to watch other people's videos, nestled in bed under the duvet. The truth was she yearned for the certainty of a home of her own. To not move around. To have her belongings at hand the whole time, the familiarity of every inch of a house and the luxury of shutting the door on a world that had always expected so much of her. She wouldn't subject her child to the constant change and physical drain of travelling the world. Even without the expectation of healing, it seemed too close to a repetition of her own childhood.

'I just want to keep things low key. Doesn't feel right to celebrate, not exactly. It's hard to explain.'

It wasn't hard to explain; it was impossible. Zach was kind and thoughtful but he hadn't lived Imogen's childhood or been bruised by the complexity of her relationship with Father. The strange thing was, she almost mourned the loss of the early years when she thought he was the most amazing man on the planet and couldn't imagine ever wanting to not be by his side. Insight can be cruel.

Zach pulled on his boots and ran his fingers through his hair in that way that meant he was biting his tongue; putting the words he didn't dare say into his body, unable to settle. 'Can we at least get out of here for a bit?'

'Okay, hang on, I'll meet you out there.' Imogen wanted to not care. Would it feel different in the morning? Would an adult version of herself walk out of the house and not turn back to check where Father was or how he would cope without her and the Rounds? She wrapped herself in her coat, glad for the extra layer.

Imogen found Father at his computer, watching YouTube videos about bird migration. The hair on the top of his head had thinned to a pale disc of scalp. His back hunched. He jotted notes into a leather-bound book. Scores of them toppled over on the floor, crammed every surface around them. She suspected he never read them back; what seemed to have purpose, had none at all. Imogen's hopes that he'd join online forums and find healthy ways to connect to others had faded. It felt awkward when they spoke. They'd lost their dance.

'I'm off out for a bit of night air. I'll see you for birthday supper. I've done the cake. Will you be all right?'

They both knew she wasn't asking about how he'd be on this one evening. They had never celebrated her birthday at exactly midnight before but the precision seemed right this time. Everything would change at the stroke of twelve.

'Things turn out just as they should, that much I know. I place trust in this world just as I have placed trust in you.'

The barbs couldn't scratch her through the wool of her coat.

'Oh and Immy, I'll head over to the cottage shortly with everything so you've nothing to concern yourself with. You two can sleep there tonight if you like, I've made the bed up.' His pet name for her and the first ever offer of she and Zach openly spending the night together. Perhaps things would change for the better. Could she allow herself to believe that?

Out by the meadow there was room to breathe again.

Imogen and Zach sat on the grass under starlight. Zach spoke excitedly about what they could see together over the next month. His lilting voice that Imogen had always loved now seemed no different to other noise pollution; as insignificant as the hum of traffic in the distance. They were on two different paths now. With each hour that passed, their diverging lines grew further apart. It wasn't Zach's fault that he hadn't noticed the degree of change in her over previous weeks – Imogen was an accomplished actress. Did she have to lose both the men she loved in order to start a new life that was truly hers?

'What if we went away for just a week instead of a month? I'd like to find a flat and get settled in. This is supposed to be the start of...' She didn't know what to call it.

Zach turned to Imogen, cupping her face as if he could better read her that way.

'I know this is weird for you, all this change but it's what you've been waiting for, isn't it? We wanted to see places together. You haven't had the chance to do what you wanted all this time.'

'Well, what if I don't want that?' She stood, needing to break their closeness in order to not weaken herself. 'I think it's all about what you want, not me.' *You're no different to Father,* she thought but didn't say. 'I'm sick of travelling. I want my own comfy chair to lounge on, to read in bed, to spend an entire Sunday in my pyjamas. It sounds stupid to you but freedom doesn't have to mean flying off all over the place, not to me anyway.'

Imogen's control was slipping. Zach jumped up and held her. He stroked her hair and spoke directly into her ear. 'It's okay, whatever you want. We can do absolutely nothing – eat, sleep, watch films. I'm sorry. I should have figured it out.' He pulled back to look at her. Imogen couldn't escape the intensity of his concern. 'Is there something else? You know you can tell me. Your dad's been a bit off with you but I guess that's understandable: his life's going to change. That's not your responsibility.'

'He wanted me to do something awful.' She wasn't supposed to say anything, not today. Now Zach would want to know more. 'All these years he told me it would be the end of the Rounds on my eighteenth birthday and that I'd get a gift. We thought he meant the inheritance, right?'

Zach's voice hardened. 'What did he mean?'

He'd always struggled to be around Father. Imogen had stood up for her family's ways repeatedly. She didn't know why. She dipped her head so that her tears fell on the ground rather than roll down her cheeks leaving evidence.

'He said it was my duty to carry on the family line. That I must get pregnant and pass on the gift to a baby girl to replace me. He said he'd bring her up.'

There was barely enough light to see by. Zach's breathing was fast and furious. 'That bastard.'

'I said no but he's been so persistent. I didn't want to tell you. We'll be away from here by tomorrow.' Imogen wished she could rewind the conversation. She should have stayed in the kitchen and counted the final hour down.

'He was trying to force you?'

'He's obsessed, you know how he is. He has ways to make me do things. But not this time.'

'That absolute bastard.' Zach was running full pelt towards The Blacksmith's Cottage before Imogen had a chance to figure out what he meant when he asked if Father had tried to force her.

29

———

CATE

I slip the key off the hook by the back door. It's early morning. Mam isn't awake yet. I have time to find what I need, even if I'm not quite sure what that is. The birds will guide me. *Psychopomps.* That's what Alana was sent to teach me. I thought she was my route to escape but instead she's my route to understand.

I avoid my usual path past the holiday house in case Alana spots me. I let her down last night. Not turning up makes it look like I was lying when I promised to meet. I can't explain to her what I learned last night. It's for me and Mam.

There's more to discover.

The Blacksmith's Cottage; that's what the one on the end of the row is called. The other cottages don't have names so they mustn't be as important. I know Mam comes down here each day but she's never let me in. This is the kind of place that secrets are buried in. I have my spade and a bucket with a meshed lid that means I can filter the soil to find clues. There's a gate with peeling black paint. It must belong to The Blacksmith's Cottage which is why it's black. I try the handle and find it isn't even locked.

The passageway is narrow. I have to concentrate on putting one foot in front of the other as straight as I can so I don't scrape my arms on the walls. I look up at the sky to tell my lungs that there's enough air to keep breathing. Halfway down, I hear a faint tapping and freeze. I check behind me but there's nobody there. I half-wish it was Alana. She'd help me and teach me more about the world. I'm cross with myself for missing the chance to ask her so many things. I didn't want her to realise how weird I was but I reckon she figured that out for herself anyhow.

I reach the back of the house. There's a yard of flagstones with weeds sprouting along each line. One day, the whole yard will erupt as all the plants pushing underneath the stones make their way to sunlight. I peer into the dirty back window but it's impossible to see anything, the curtains must be drawn. Over a low wall I can see into the next yard which is just as neglected. Who are the villagers that Mam takes fresh produce to? I never saw them. I never asked. I never questioned why they didn't leave Halham because neither did I.

Dig, dig, sieve, sieve. I set up a routine that feels good. Little stones get trapped in the lid of the bucket along with twigs and a snail's shell. It takes a long time to find anything on an archaeological dig. I must be patient. I don't know what I'm looking for. Buried treasure or buried bones?

I try out a chant while I dig and sieve; *The Rounds*. When Mam finished her story last night, I asked her if the phrase had capital letters and felt a thrill when she said she supposed it did. It's the kind of magic that could belong to me.

TheRoundsTheRoundstheroundstheroundza. Repetition melts the name into a mystical word – *roundza*. All this time I thought it was only me that was different but it's Mam too. She spent all her time travelling and using her healing powers to cure people. It seems kind of amazing but I could tell from

Mam's voice it had been full of pain and darkness. It sounded like she had tiny knives in the back of her throat as she described those visits. I felt them in my own throat as she spoke. They've left behind one hundred tiny cuts to my larynx.

Zach said the healing wasn't real. He thinks that grandfather invented Mam's powers. Mam said he got that wrong but her voice wasn't as sure as her words. It's up to me to use my scientist skills to test myself but I'm not sure how. Mam isn't unwell so I can't try to make her better. There's no way to know for sure.

A robin's spring song calls out from above me. That's when I remember what Alana taught me: birds can be messengers of the dead. My grandfather could be trying to tell me about the gift. Or he could be trying to tell Mam that he got it wrong and he's sorry. I've been digging in the ground for answers when they could be much higher up than that.

I run to the back of the yard to get a better view of the roof. A chimney sticks out at the side of the house all the way to the sky. Goldfinches chirrup and flutter around the chimney stack and dip across the back window. Yellow flashes on their wings. Some goldfinches migrate to Spain in the winter but ours never leave. They've been gathering clues all year round so they can tell me something. This is the house. I knew it. Not the soil or the yard; I need to go inside. There are different ways to bury things.

At the front of the house, I take a quick look to see if Mam or Alana are in the distance. There's nobody about. I've never used a key before so it takes a few tries to open the front door. It creaks gently as I push it. There's a door ahead and steep stairs to my right made from stone. The ceiling hangs low. It's as dark as evening; a house trapped in twilight. I need to get as close to the birds as possible so they can give me their message – I need to be upstairs where they gather by the windows.

The stairs are not made of straight lines, they curve around the corner. The walls aren't flat like ours. Every surface is bumpy and rough. There is one room at either end of the house and a cupboard in between. The front room is a bedroom. It's so dusty it feels like my tongue is fuzzy from breathing in. The bedding has a faded pattern. There's an old leather suitcase. I lift the lid a little but it's empty. Nobody sleeps here.

The cupboard in between contains a huge cylinder. It's warm to the touch. There are quiet clunks from inside as if something tiny is tapping to get out. Perhaps it's a human nest. There could be eggs or babies incubating inside but I can't see any opening to check the contents. Maybe it's where I was made so Mam didn't have to touch me on her insides unlike the pregnant farm animals whose babies roll inside them then slither out, covered in blood and glue. I hold my hands against the warmth for a little longer.

The back room isn't a bathroom as I expected. I switch on the light, which hangs from the middle of the room covered by a floral upside-down basket. The room is rectangular with wooden floorboards. A patterned rug tries to cover them but can't quite manage.

Air seeps through the sides of the window even though it's shut. I hold my hand over the cracks in the wall, letting the outside into the inside. A goldfinch flickers past. I can hear its family chattering.

Me and Mam used to play a game called *Seek the Stone*. We'd take it in turns to hide Mam's deep purple amethyst that was the size of my hand, spiky and sparkly. Whoever hid it would shout "hotter" or "colder" depending how near the one searching for it was to the correct place. Now, the excited goldfinches call that I'm getting warmer. That means I'm close to finding something or someone.

I should have asked Alana more about messages from the

dead that travel via birds. I know some of their language. It's not the same as looking up words in the French-English dictionary; I have to let my insides translate and see what they tell me. I pay careful attention to the trill of the goldfinches but it doesn't work if I try too hard. My insides don't tell me anything other than a gurgle from missing breakfast. Mam will be ready by now and wondering where I am. I need to hurry up. Maybe all the birds could say for sure was that this room is important.

There are mismatched wooden tables covered with little cardboard boxes and a length of cotton wool. Underneath the tables are larger cardboard boxes which are taped shut. I heave one out and pick at the thick brown tape, wishing I didn't bite my nails so low. A corner peels up and I'm careful to act much more slowly than I want to; if I rush, I'll leave evidence that I've been in here. I pull up the cardboard lips a little. The box is full of hardback books. The top few are about war, butterflies and wild flowers. I pull the butterfly book left and right to ease it up. It has a maroon cover with two gold butterflies pressed into the hard surface. The pages smell like another time and place. *British Butterflies: Every Native Species, London, George Routledge and Sons, 1867*. There are illustrations of species I've never seen, grouped together on pages as if they were caught, pressed and put to eternal sleep together.

I replace the book and nudge the heavy box back under the table. I'm not sure how my grandfather would be able to communicate to me. Being dead means you can't speak or move.

I gently lift the lid on the smallest box then nearly drop it. Hair! A curl of hair that is golden brown. It doesn't look like the white hair I saw on the photo of my grandfather. I slip it out of the box and into my pocket. I'll call it a Treasure. The other boxes are slightly longer. I open one after the other but they are empty apart from cotton wool. There's an indentation of where something previously lay on top of the soft white bed in each. How tiny are babies when they're first born?

'What are you trying to tell me, Grandfather?'

Silence. The birds have abandoned me.

'I don't understand and now I need to go but I think there's something you wanted me to know. Is that right?'

A clang replies. Not the faint tapping of the nest in the cupboard but a louder response, like a metallic shout.

'Have I got the gift? Is it real?'

Silence for a few beats. Then the clang again. One, two, three, four, five, six, seven, eight, nine of them. That's the answer. I have what I came for even though I haven't decoded it yet. I run down the stairs, pull the front door behind me, and rush home, all the while counting my steps in sequences of nine.

30

—————

IMOGEN

NOW

It's only morning but already a tension headache wraps itself across the bridge of Imogen's nose and tightens its band around her head. Zach should be back in his van but he's inches away on the sofa.

'I want to understand your life here. You look at me in that wild way like I'm here to wreck it but that isn't it at all. Let me in a little.'

Oh, she knows what happens when you let people in. Once the door is opened, that person takes up residence in thoughts and dreams until it becomes impossible to separate out the self from the other.

Imogen recalls a time when the world of the Rounds and Father faded to grey compared to her moments with Zach. She'd craved him. Before Zach, her body felt almost disgusting to her; she tried not to inhabit that which others desired and drained, preferring to live inside her mind. But with Zach, touch was transformed. No longer the sting of strangers' germs, the heat of their disease or the scratching of nails into her hand. His touch was warmth on her back, his thigh hot against hers, his teeth on her neck with a different type of pressure.

'I've had too much of that damson wine last night. It's not even nice.'

Zach scrunches up his nose. 'It was okay. I mean, I'd rather have had a beer to be honest.'

Imogen is slightly unsteady as she gets to her feet to clear away evidence of the night before. Why had she ordered the wine from a neighbour's farm when she'd rather have a gin and tonic? 'It's all part of the role, I guess. It seemed wholesome, the kind of thing I should be drinking.'

'Where does the *should* come from? You can choose how you live now. There's nobody here to judge or pressure you.'

Imogen slams the washed glass down harder than she intended. 'Apart from you. Are you here to rescue me? Fix me? Is that what you think? Because that's not what I need. I'm doing the best I can and I never said it was perfect, but it's good enough. Cate's happy. She's safe. We don't need you here.'

Zach leans back on the worktop like he's avoiding fire breathed out from her mouth. 'I know you don't need me, but could you make a little room for me, for now? Cate seems like a lovely girl. I'd like to have the chance to get to know her more.'

It's such a reasonable request and yet it feels dangerous.

'You're pushing me too fast.'

'Imogen, look at me instead of the floor, please. I'm here but it's like you won't let me be. You don't have to do this all on your own. You say Cate is happy in this life – but are you? All those years that you looked forward to having your freedom yet you're still here, at Halham, doing nothing for yourself.'

Perhaps men are missing something; a tiny, vital part of the brain. That's why they can avoid responsibility, ignore those they love, choose to interpret the world to suit themselves. That's why a gene for healing skips right past them, switched off until it's activated in female offspring.

'I do the thing that matters most in the world; I give my

daughter the best life possible despite it costing me my freedom.'

'You think you've given her freedom.'

'But what? I can tell you have more to say. You don't have to treat me like I'm breakable: just say it.'

Zach's mouth tightens. 'You think you've given her freedom, but you've created a prison for both of you.'

He may as well have punched her. Everything hurts. Her wrists, the small of her back, the pull of muscles down the backs of her legs. The tension headache is morphing into a migraine. She can't think in a straight line. 'I need to go back to bed. I can't carry on with this discussion. You need to go.'

Imogen wishes to keep hold of her flash of anger and the strength she can use from it. But it's extinguished by the concern on Zach's face. It's strange to have another adult present, to step out of parenting mode and see the edges of what it feels like to be a person in her own right.

How many times did Zach gently try to persuade her to tell Father she was not doing the Rounds when she was sixteen and seventeen? Every time he tried to support her, Imogen would snap at how he didn't understand. In the end, he stopped suggesting she put in any boundaries with Father. She knew what he thought but chose to ignore it. She wasn't good at being cared for.

'I'll come back later then to see Cate?'

Imogen wants to take his hand and lead him upstairs. She wants to be held and feel the heaviness of him on her, his gentle touch soothing all the hurt.

'No. I think you should go back home. This has all got out of hand. We need some time for things to settle here.'

Zach doesn't reply.

Imogen turns to the window and grips the basin, its

porcelain cool against her skin, until the door clicks shut and he is gone.

31

CATE

When I sneak back home, something has changed. Mam is in busy mode but I can see the grey cloud inside her. Flashes of lightning flicker in the whites of her eyes.

'I was going to take my book to the field to read. Is that okay?'

Mam slaps both hands on her thighs as she stands. 'Just to let you know, Zach has gone home. We need a bit of time for ourselves.'

She carries on talking but I can't let the words in. I'm close to breaking the code of Mam, The Blacksmith's Cottage, the secrets of Halham. I don't know why but I think Zach needs to be here. He's the only one who knows Mam properly, not the acting she does for me. I need to know more about the healing powers. He might understand why my grandfather wanted to tell me the number nine.

'No, Mam! It isn't time for him to go yet.'

It's as though I haven't spoken. She starts packing up some gardening equipment in a bag. I usually love watching Mam at work, the certainty of which items belong together for a task. Today's bag is being packed for moving seedlings from indoors to outdoors. She speaks without looking away from what she's doing. 'Don't you miss things being the way they usually are? The way they should be?'

Yes.

No.

I wonder what it would feel like to fall down a very deep hole? When I fell off my bike or out of Brown's arms, it was as if I didn't have time to realise until I was already on the ground. But if there's an earthquake in Halham and the land splits into two, a crack might form with a crevice all the way to the centre of the earth. What would go through my head as I dived deeper towards the liquid rock below?

'Did you tell Zach to go?'

Mam flushes and her little red blood cells have given me the answer. There's no point in arguing. I can't lose my chance at a line to the past. Before I've decided what to do, my body is running as fast as it can, taking me to the lane, *please be there, please be there, please still be there.*

I haven't put my shoes back on after pretending I'd only just got out of bed. My feet smack against stones. I don't stop.

I turn the bend into the lane and see the blue and white van. My feet don't hurt one bit, like I'm running on the surface of a pretend lake in the virtual reality world.

'Zach!'

Why do I want to see him? Why isn't me and Mam enough? It is. It is. We haven't finished talking, that's all. He's my route to know Mam more; to be even closer than ever.

Zach steps out of his van. His hair is messy and his eyelids are swollen. 'Why don't you come in for a bit?'

I talk fast so he doesn't have time to interrupt or call Mam or ask me to leave so he can drive away forever. I tell him that I need to know all about Mam, and Halham, and healing, and grandfather, and the number nine, and the armadillos in the

United States of America, and what it feels like to be flying through the air with your house far below.

'Your mum has asked me to leave. I thought I'd give her a bit of time. Sometimes she needs her space to think things through. I'll have to go because this is her home. I don't have the right to be here without an invitation.'

I think about all the people waiting outside our gates. Poorly people. I imagine Zach standing outside, rattling the gates that Mam refuses to open as she turns up the dial on her music and tells me to run out to the daisies until all the commotion passes.

'I don't want you to go yet. Please stay. Find a way to make Mam allow it, she won't listen to me. But she'll listen to you, maybe. She's known you a long time.' I don't mention the photo of them together when they were young with their faces pressed against one another. There was no room in the picture for anyone else.

'Your mum needs time. Maybe you do, too, I get that now.'

He doesn't realise that it doesn't matter what I want or don't want. Mam is the writer and the director. Only she decides what will happen next.

Halham isn't a village, Zach explains. Halham means *house of health* in Old English and it was grandfather's inherited estate. All of it. The playground is the bottom of our huge garden. The cottages used to belong to workers when the family was wealthy and owned all the land. It's the grounds of Mam's old home and I've never left it.

The birds knew it but I didn't.

There's even more Zach could explain to me. I could ask him every single question from my list. He said he'd answer anything at all.

I'm not ready yet. I don't want to leave Mam out.

'Are you okay?'

I don't know. Am I okay? Do I have Mam's old gift to cure people? Or have I stayed at home for no reason at all?

Lose-lose.

'I want Mam.'

Zach takes his phone from his pocket and presses a button. 'It's okay, she's here in the van. I haven't left yet. Do you want to speak to her?' He passes me his phone.

It's strange to hear Mam's voice coming through the speaker, not quite the same tone as usual. 'Thank goodness, I've been looking for you.'

'Mam, please let Zach stay a couple of days. It's not time yet. I'm sorry for running, my feet wanted to find him.'

She asks me to pass the phone back to Zach. He turns his body away from me. At the back of his neck, the hair is slightly wavy like the underneath of my hair. I wonder if I'll be able to remember what he smells like when he's gone? There's a blue T-shirt folded on the floor next to me. It's too big to scrunch up and place under my dress. Instead, I take his black pen and slip it into my pocket.

'Okay, it looks like I'll stay for a couple more days. Your mum wants you back home now.'

Mam changed her mind about something. Is that because I asked or because Zach did? I have an ache in my stomach like I haven't eaten for days.

'Your shoes appear to have evaporated.'

I laugh and notice that one of my toes is bleeding. It doesn't matter. I want to go home and have the triangle of us for two more days. Then Zach will go back to his own house and everything will go back to the way it should be.

Won't it?

32

IMOGEN

NOW

It has been so long since Imogen has allowed herself to think about her own mother, that she can't quite picture her. In place of a true image, she finds a pantomime version; a screeching fishwife as a minor character, existing only as a foil to the hero of the story. It had always felt as if giving love to her mother would dilute that which she had for Father.

It takes over half an hour for Imogen to find a single photograph that has her mother in. If she buried the photograph box for one hundred years, on excavating it, the new owner would presume that a widower and his daughter had lived at Halham. What cruel exclusion from her own family. No wonder her mother hadn't maintained contact. One bitterly cold winter night, Father had warmed himself with whisky and told Imogen that her mother had moved to France. She didn't ask any questions so as not to appear treacherous. It's peculiar to look back and see how reasonable it would have been to enquire further. How the far more treacherous thing was to write off the woman who birthed her and act as if she had never existed. Perhaps her mother is still in France, waiting for a letter to invite her back home.

In the photograph, Imogen's mother is standing next to her beloved bicycle. She's squinting into sunlight, her face creased by a reaction to its fierce brightness that day. Imogen had forgotten that it was her mother who had offered to teach her to ride when she was about eight years old. Imogen remembers the day as clearly as if she'd stepped back into it.

'I bought these stabilisers from the hardware shop, simple enough to put on your back wheels. It's about time you learnt; these will make it easier.'

Imogen didn't understand what was in the brown paper bag but was immediately suspicious of the idea as it hadn't come from Father. 'I don't need them. I'm going to practise on Sunday.'

Imogen made it sound like a plan had already been agreed with Father. She didn't need to use his name, that was a given. It might upset him if there was something important that he hadn't thought about. Besides, she thought it sounded like the kind of thing a baby needed. Imogen was sure she'd be excellent at cycling once she tried it.

'Well, why don't I put them on for your first few tries, I could take you out on the lane for half an hour before I make dinner?' Her mother's hopeful face made her uncomfortable; she preferred the familiarity of her scowl.

The awful squeeze in her stomach started which came when she got things wrong. Surely she'd be able to ride but what if she fell off? Her mother may say *I told you so* to Father, with evidence that Imogen was just a normal little girl like she'd told him all along.

'I'm going on Sunday and I don't need those. You can get your money back if you return them without opening the packet.'

There, that felt better; a solution had been found. No need for her mother to be upset if she got her money back. Imogen ran off to her room to read, unaware that she would end up with cuts, bruises and humiliation from weeks of practising on her bike with Father without stabilisers in place.

Her mother had tried to help. She can see that now. In fact, cycling may have been the one thing that brought her mother contentment. She'd spend hours out on the country lanes. Father never asked her where she'd been or what she'd seen, so Imogen didn't either. It suited them all to keep busy, so it seemed. Had her mother tried to find something they could do together? Was it out of duty or a real effort to connect? Imogen runs her finger over the photograph. It doesn't even look like Mother, her face screwed up in the sun this way. What must it have been like to be constantly rejected by her own child? It was hard to say which came first: her mother's sharp edges or Imogen's refusal to let her be a parent.

A belief in the sacredness of a duo is hard to shake off. She heard her mother's harsh tone stream out of her own mouth when she argued with Zach. Imogen can see the good in him as well as potential for enrichment of Cate's life with him in it, but his presence feels like a threat to something sacred. She doesn't know how to create room for anyone else without feeling dread. What is it she's afraid of?

Imogen washes the dishes in the sink so she has something to do with her hands. The scent of the washing-up liquid is harsh and unnatural but the warmth of the water holds her. She pulls out the plug and watches the water circle down the drain. She recalls Father telling her that in Australia, water drains in the opposite direction; the laws of the planet reversed simply by being in another place.

33

CATE

I don't like how much Zach looks at Mam. He tries to hide it but I know all about keeping close watch on her.

'Zach would like to find out more about our life here, I thought you could show him what you get up to in Halham before he leaves tomorrow?'

As we pass Mam on our way out, Zach places his hand on her arm for a moment. My legs heat up like they need to march so I take the lead down towards the field. I can't think out loud with Zach trailing right behind me. He changes the way things are just by being here.

Zach jogs to catch up with me.

'Right then, team leader, where to first?'

I don't have a plan yet. I want to show him how great life is here so that he knows me and Mam are fine and he can leave us to it. But I don't want him loving it too much. What if he decides to stay longer? What if he starts to believe he's not an Outsider and wants to live here? There's no room for him.

'Have you got your own house to go back to or just the van?'

'I have a room in a house I share with some friends. The van is my escape mechanism for when I need some time by myself

195

or to be somewhere different for a while. Do you know what I mean?'

I think about lying down flat on the field, listening to the land, or curling up inside the climbing frame, or lifting my elasticated bed-sheet and crawling under, being careful not to pull it up from the mattress so it holds me tight. 'Maybe.'

I don't want to show him all my special places. I think that would make him fall in love with Halham. I don't want him to love Halham. Or love Mam.

Mam told me about love potions in stories. If you drink one, you fall in love with the next person you see. The magic makes everything they do or say seem amazing. They are the most beautiful person in the world and you feel like you'd die without them near you. She said that eventually the magic potion wears off. You notice how irritating their habits are, or that you don't like the way they breathe, or that they only ever talk about themselves. Perhaps the potion doesn't wear off if you don't see your beloved, perhaps it takes longer to fade. I'd like to grind some seeds, petals and leaves to make an antidote. But there's no need because Zach is going far away tomorrow.

'Are we heading somewhere in particular?'

I wonder what Zach would be interested in. He's rather different to Mam. He seems to like the small details like me, not needing them to have a practical purpose other than to be different.

'Would you like to see the half-and-half tree?'

'I absolutely would.'

Zach has the kind of smile that doesn't hold any worry at the edges.

We curve off the path to get to the apple tree that sits with its cousins at the edge of our field. I didn't want to draw Mam's attention to it so never shared its name before. I bite my thumbnail to stop myself from telling Zach all about the tree; I want to see what he thinks. I want to use our trip to be a Zachologist.

'Here it is.' I point at the right side of the tree which is covered with blushed-white blossom. 'Half,' then to the left side which has dead, bare branches, 'and half.'

Zach moves closer, looking from left to right and back again.

'Wow, I see why you gave it such a perfect name. It's half flowering – I suppose there will be apples there in time – and the other half has nothing at all. Both parts are the same tree.'

I wriggle my toes at Zach's attention to what I've shown him. He doesn't ask me any questions like what it makes me think about or how it makes me feel. Zach doesn't use the tree as a clue to check if I'm being normal or happy enough. Instead, it's me looking for clues about him. He doesn't realise I'm being a scientist of people.

'I was wondering what you'd make of the half-and-half tree,' I say, deciding it's unfair not to be clear about my interest.

'I'm glad you showed me, I could have easily not noticed it amongst the other trees. You know Halham so well. I suppose the left side needed pruning. Without the care, that side of it has died while the other half thrives. I think the tree is unusual and rather beautiful. But I feel a little bit sad for that side without the flowers, that won't have the apples growing soon.'

'Can you like something and be sad about it at the same time?'

That doesn't fit with the feelings chart Mam used to have up on the wall in the study for me to point to. Sad, happy, angry, scared, anxious with cartoon faces and a thermometer to show how strong the feeling was out of ten. We added our own words: tired, hungry, and busy brain for when the thoughts got too whizzy to concentrate. But I never chose more than one answer.

'Yes, I think we often have a mix of feelings about the same thing. Or the same person. For example, in thirty seconds, you're going to feel both impressed and annoyed with me.'

I don't know what to say. Can Zach read behind my eyes too or is that a joke?

'Race you to the fence,' shouts Zach, already running, whooping as he goes.

'Cheat! I wasn't ready!' I run too, irritated about his trick but also laughing.

We then sit with our backs against the fence. I pant with my head turned away so Zach can't see. I run my fingers along the tips of grass blades so they tickle.

'You know I care about your mum, but I'll never, ever get between the two of you. I can see how special you are to each other. That won't change. But you might find that there's room for more in your life; more people, more places.' He copies me by running his hand over the grass. 'When you're ready, I mean.'

My feelings don't know what to do. Green and orange and red mix together into a sludgy brown. Zach slips off his shoes and wiggles his toes in the grass. I do the same.

'Can you tell me about France and the United States of America?'

For a moment, Zach gives me that soft look that's usually for Mam. 'Of course! Shall I just describe it or would you like me to look up some pictures on my phone, too?'

'Pictures, please.' I bite my lip. 'And, can you show me how to find them?'

Zach nods and I press record on the camera of my mind to watch this scene again later and decide if it deserves to go on a list.

I try not to think about dead branches reaching across to shake blossom from the healthy side of the tree.

34

———————

IMOGEN

NOW

The difference between faith and science is disintegrating. Imogen sits on the back step of her house, staring at her hands as if they could hold an answer. Faint echoes of heat and pain from withdrawing strangers' viruses and mutant cells remain.

It's not the first time she's wondered about the power of placebo. There were a couple of years when she scoured every scientific article she could find on the topic, alongside developmental psychology studies on childhood imagination and even delusional disorders shared within families. By then, she was five years into living away from the world with Cate. It had been too late to change, and besides, the stakes seemed too high to risk if she was wrong. She never wanted her little girl to feel responsible for the health and happiness of others.

From the house, there are two routes down to the bottom of Halham estate. Imogen always takes the path along the field but could just as easily follow Cate's favoured route, along the hedgerows, past the holiday house.

Imogen gathers the food and drink items and heads towards the row of cottages, along the same path as usual. She wants to drown out the cruel line Zach threw at her but it won't leave. *You think you've given her freedom, but you've created a prison.* She would never forgive him for that. She's not the same as Father, in fact she's done everything she could to be the opposite. It came with a cost as all choices do.

Today seems different to Imogen; her autopilot has failed. She feels every dagger of emotion. There's no way to hide the truth any longer. Zach and Cate will be back home soon and she must decide how to break the news to both of them.

In The Blacksmith's Cottage, Imogen lays out the food along with medication. With her numbness stripped back, every sense is crammed with nostalgia. Her hazy history comes into sharp focus. The smell of the place; musty and decrepit. The orange glow of the sunlight through faded curtains. The clunk of an old boiler as she rinses a mug under the tap. What she doesn't hear – hasn't heard since the night she became an adult – is the sound of Father's voice.

She doesn't want to go into the living room; not in this vulnerable state. The name of it is a cruel joke. Memories flood back as real as if she could time travel. There was no way Cate could have known what happened, despite her imagination conjuring up a scene so similar.

Once Imogen realised Zach's misinterpretation, she had run to the cottage, planning to clarify. If she had spoken up immediately or grabbed Zach by his shirt, perhaps she could have prevented it all. She heard Zach shouting before she entered the house, the front door wide open. The two men in her life had barely acknowledged each other's existence until this point.

'You're sick! You should never be near Imogen again!'

Father froze. He was a gentle man who used his words over fists. But he was no pushover. 'Stand down, lad, I think we need to talk this through. Here's Imogen now.'

That did nothing to defuse the situation. Zach ignored her, his face wracked with pain. 'She told me what you wanted to do to her.'

Why didn't Imogen's mouth form the explanation that was needed? Father wanted her to get pregnant, not to impregnate her himself. He was misguided but not a monster.

As usual, Father heard what he expected to, not paying attention to what was actually said. 'It's the right thing to do. It's for the Rounds.'

It happened so fast. Zach's left arm swung through the air; Father dropped. Imogen ran over, unable to speak, other than a breathless 'no'. She meant, *No, he'd never do that, no, you got it wrong, no, I should have stopped you, no, this can't happen.*

'Let's get out of here.'

Zach didn't realise that one punch can be enough. He wasn't a violent man; he'd only tried to protect her.

The time. Why had she looked up at the clock? The party was set for midnight, to mark the start of her adulthood. It was one minute to twelve.

This is the image that haunts her. Not the punch, not the blood, not Father's face; the large hand of the clock that was not yet pointing straight upwards.

She didn't touch him.

Imogen had sixty seconds to cradle Father's head and extinguish the blood clot that had formed with the blow to his skull from the hard floor. Instead, she knelt beside him. She'd checked that clock. There was no denying it. It wasn't panic or a lack of awareness of the urgency. She had sixty seconds of using her gift for the final time for the man she'd loved most in the whole world for most of her life but did nothing. There was no explanation for it. No excuse.

Click. The minute hand moved into place. She was eighteen years old.

'Zach, he's not coming round. I'll call an ambulance.'

Reality sank in and Zach's face drained of blood. He hadn't meant any harm, just a warning.

'Go. Get out of here. Now. I'll sort it.'

'I can't leave you.'

'Go now, I don't want to see you in a cell.'

Imogen spoke to the paramedic over the phone, explaining how her father had been hit in the face by a door and whacked his head on the stone floor. She followed all orders without hesitation. She was an adult from that moment and felt the heaviness of its implications. Imogen cradled Father in her lap, telling him it would be okay even though it never would be again. She imagined her baby being flooded with stress hormones, unable to escape her poisonous womb.

'Get out of here, go to the sea. Contact me in a few days. Pretend you were never here, that we broke up earlier today and so you left. They're on their way, please go, they're bound to ask questions.'

Zach hesitated.

'For me. Go.'

As usual, though reluctantly, he did as she asked.

The stroke had done its damage. Zach was out of the way. Toria was long gone. It was just Imogen and her baby now. Imogen, her baby, and the guilt.

Imogen pushes the door open to the living room, the same as she has every day for over a decade. When Cate was little, she'd set her up in the bouncer in the kitchen but never brought her in here. This was Imogen's penance. Or perhaps it was Father's.

Even in the spring daytime, the room remains as gloomy as its occupant insists on.

'Hmmph.' Father acknowledges her presence in the only way he can since aphasia caused by the blood clot robbed him of his lyrical language. He taps his stick against the piping in protest.

'I know, I'm so sorry I'm late today but I'm here now.'

35

CATE

When we arrive back at the house, everything is the same but different.

'How was your day?'

'It was okay. We took a walk and looked at nature.'

'Sounds perfect for Zach, to distract him from the blue of the sea with all the green we have to show off around here!' Mam tries to make her voice light but it sounds off, like when I try to make a D-major chord on the keyboard but my finger slips onto the wrong key.

Zach removes his shoes and places them by the back door. I don't know how soon it will be before he'll have them back on. I try to read Mam's face but her mask is fixed tightly in place.

I want to run to the field and lie with the daisies until my blackbird comes. I have secrets to tap out onto the earth. But I daren't leave Mam and Zach alone.

'Did she pester you with hundreds of questions?' Mam's nervous that she's been left out. I'm glad now that I kept my notebook in my bag rather than asking Zach all my questions. Me and Mam are still a team.

'No, not at all. We just paid attention to what was around us and talked about other places I've been to.'

Mam's lips thin. I need her to know she's still my best person. I wish I could make her shoulders jiggle when she laughs.

I don't know how to make things work between us with Zach here, too. The triangle of us has three sharp points. The line between me and Mam is gold because it's number one. There's a fuzzy line between me and Zach who don't know each other yet. But what about between Mam and Zach?

Could it ever feel right, three of us instead of two?

A triangle is the most stable shape. I remember that from geometry.

'Cate, are you listening to me?'

'I was just wondering what colour line there is between you two. I can't see it.'

Mam sighs. She doesn't like it when I tell her the truth of what's in my head. I didn't mean to but being with Zach stopped me from being careful.

He looks between the two of us. 'I wonder what the different colours would mean? Seems you're trying to figure out something important?'

'Don't encourage it, Zach. You're the one saying she needs to live in the outside world one day. How do you think that would go down beyond these four walls? She'd be bullied the second she opened her mouth.'

'Isn't that more reason to try to understand her world? She's trying to work out who she is and what the world is like without enough information or experience.'

'Don't you think I've spent years trying to get this right? To consider what to explain and when for the best? You spend five minutes here and think you know better than me.'

They talk across me as if I'm not here. The gold line

between me and Mam starts to get thinner and lighter. Perhaps I'm fading into invisibility. Like grandfather.

I haven't told Mam about ghosts and birds. The dead find a way to communicate. The number nine is important to him.

'I know about grandfather. He can't settle into death because something bad happened and it hasn't been sorted out. The birds have been trying to tell me but I wasn't listening properly. We need to make it right so he can be at peace.'

Zach looks as shocked as when I hit him. Mam grips the back of the dining-room chair. I switch my attention to the sounds outside; the chirp of sparrows, a machine-gun robin, the whistle and trill of my blackbird. They agree with me, relieved at last to be heard.

'Cate, there's something me and your mother need to talk to you about. Why don't we all go and sit down?'

I follow Zach over to the sofa, each of us perched on one end while Mam takes the armchair.

'Actually, I was hoping to write Zach a letter about all this after he left. But I suppose it's better this way.' Mam's body is floppy and older now. She tips her head back on the leather and brings her legs up crossed in front of her like she's doing yoga. 'A long time ago, Zach misunderstood something I told him about your grandfather. He acted before I could explain.'

Zach tries to interrupt but Mam holds her hand up without even looking at him. 'Let me finish. Both of you. It's never right to hit but Zach was very upset. He hit your grandfather, just once. I arrived as it happened and I can't explain why I didn't stop him; it was like I was moving under water and couldn't react in time. Your grandfather fell to the floor and banged his head. That caused a haemorrhage – a bleed on his brain.'

'I'm so, so sorry, I've never forgiven myself...'

'Stop. Just stop and for once listen to me. You and Father never really listened. It's not you who should be sorry, it's me.'

She turns to Cate. 'Your grandfather isn't a ghost, sweetheart. He had a massive stroke, lost some movement down one side and his power of speech. But he didn't die. I should have told you, Zach, once you phoned from Cornwall but it was complicated. I was already pregnant. I decided what was for the best and I stuck with it.'

I hold back from the caws that want to pour from the back of my throat, as wild and cross as the jackdaw.

'My grandfather is still in Halham, that's what the birds were telling me. He can't speak so they tried to speak for him.'

Mam holds her head in her hands and cries. I wait for the argument to start up again but Zach jumps up to kneel in front of her, holding her tight.

I wait. I count to one hundred and press each finger in turn against the soft pad of my thumb so I don't interrupt or speak too soon. The blackbird asks me who I thought the milk and food was for all these years or why I never went down to The Blacksmith's Cottage with Mam. I hadn't really thought about it.

I've waited long enough. Mam's head is up now. She's wiping her face with a tissue. Zach hasn't taken his eyes off her.

'He always wanted to stay at Halham. But I couldn't let him know about you. So, I moved him to The Blacksmith's Cottage and cared for him there. At first, I used my inheritance to buy in discreet carers but he didn't like it so I took over. He can move around a little on the ground floor but he needs me every day. It's gone on so long that we're both used to it.'

I hadn't been alone in The Blacksmith's Cottage, someone had been there, listening. Not a ghost but an old man who spends all his life in Halham, just like me.

'Can I ask one question?'

She nods, dabbing underneath her eyes.

'If the healing really works, how come you couldn't make him better?'

The curtains behind Mam's eyes are shut so I can't see what she's thinking.

'I was eighteen when I called the ambulance.' I open my mouth but I've used up my one question already. Mam continues, sounding more like her normal self now. Her battery is gaining power. Mine is nearly empty. 'The healing didn't work anymore because I was an adult.'

Zach lays his hand on Mam's shoulder. I'm alone on the sofa.

'Why don't you get some rest while me and your mum have a chance to talk things through.'

'Yes, go upstairs now, Cate. We can sort things out more tomorrow. I love you very much, you know that.'

My grandfather doesn't know about me. Mam never takes me out on her trips. Zach only just found out about me.

That's why I've always felt unreal; I only exist in Halham.

I'm suddenly too tired to think. The water in my cells spills out, filling my eyes and ears. My body softens and falls into a pair of arms that carry me up the stairs. I float down a river to the open sea.

36

IMOGEN

NOW

Imogen watches her daughter sleep, curled in on herself like she's still in utero. It's almost six in the morning. There's an agitation in her bones that won't let her make the most of this moment. She's been in and out of sleep on the sofa with Zach by her side. God knows how he managed to forgive her. He has a skill for living in the present moment; letting go of the past as if what's done is done. There's a long road of repair ahead. She doesn't yet know what she wants it to look like.

'Mam?' Cate's hair is strewn over her face. She slept in yesterday's clothes after being too wiped out to change into pyjamas last night.

'Morning. Shall I get you breakfast?'

Cate shakes her head. 'When are the people in the holiday house leaving?'

Could she have avoided this by allowing Cate to make friends here in a controlled way? How stupid to underestimate the yearnings of an adolescent.

'I'm sorry, they left yesterday. It was a short rental.' Imogen doesn't mention the pink envelope with glitter that is folded into her handbag. Perhaps she will. She needs to loosen the ties that have bound her girl too tightly.

'I want to tell you something. I borrowed the key from by the back door and went to The Blacksmith's Cottage before you told me about my grandfather. I was looking for clues because my friend taught me about ghosts and birds. Anyway, it was strange in there. I think there's an incubator in the cupboard. Is that where you grew me?'

Imogen's knees weaken. She sits on the edge of the bed next to Cate. What has she done to Cate's mind by keeping her away from society? She mustn't shame her or close her down but encourage her to share her world.

'Tell me what you saw.'

'The warm cylinder in between two rooms upstairs. It was a bit like a human nest. I was wondering if that's how you grew me and if you'd make me a baby brother or sister one day?'

'Oh Cate, that's the boiler. It heats up the water for the house. That isn't how you were made. I've been meaning to explain things, but...'

But what? She'd packed so many layers of protection around Cate that it seemed impossible to peel any away. 'What else did you see there?'

Cate bites her bottom lip. Imogen pays careful attention not to mirror her expression. She forces the muscles in her face to let down their guard.

'Boxes everywhere. The birds told me to go into that room and I tried to ask the ghost of grandfather if the healing power was real or not, and the answer is the number nine.'

Imogen focuses on her daughter's eyes; the light hazel she inherited from Zach. She must stay connected to the moment however much she feels like fleeing the room.

'How do you know the answer is nine?'

Cate jumps up and grabs her pen, takes it to the radiator and taps nine times.

Father's stick against the pipes – his preferred way to gain Imogen's attention. She bought him an iPad with a special communication program with set phrases but he rarely uses it for that purpose. He spends his time reading and watching videos of the world he no longer inhabits in between naps. That damned stick against the pipe is a sound that haunts her but she accepts he can choose his way of being heard.

'You asked if the healing was real?'

Nine chimes. Nine syllables. *It is if you believe it to be.*

'Your grandfather has his own way of answering questions that isn't really an answer at all.' How many of his patterns had replayed through her own behaviours?

'I don't know how to find out if I have the gift or if I want to know.'

The world slows down. This is the moment Imogen had been dreading and yet there's some relief in it finally coming to pass. Cate continues, speaking in the fast, precise way she does when she has rehearsed something. Perhaps that's the only way she has been able to get her point across before being shut down.

'There are three bedrooms in the holiday house.'

Zach said to pay attention to what Cate is trying to figure out when she says odd things.

'Hmm, that's right. What does that make you think about?'

'Well, there's enough for six people if you squeeze but we don't need that many. I don't mind having the strange bed with two levels. You could have the large room with space for another person, which has lots of light and its own toilet. And so, then there's one room left.'

Does she mean for Zach or Father?

Imogen isn't ready for this. She has put one foot forward and needs time to steady herself. She exhales her tension away.

'I need to think things through. We can make some changes but I don't want to rush. Let's take one day at a time.' Imogen is advising herself as much as her daughter. 'What would you like to do today that would make it special?'

The images flood in, turning her fears into visions – Cate rushing into the living room at The Blacksmith's Cottage causing Father to have another stroke, or Cate packing her bags, determined to leave Halham forever with Zach to start a new life by the sea. But she has to start asking Cate what she wants rather than always deciding for her.

'Can me and you spend today in the top places in Halham? I have a list.'

Imogen can't help but laugh, engulfed in love. 'I bet you have. I hope it's in alphabetical order.'

Cate chirrups away non-stop as they do a tour of the estate in the order that matters to her: climbing frame, corner shop, field, gates, hedgerows, holiday house, vegetable patch, view of Hart Hill.

At the hedgerow, Imogen shows Cate an app that can label any species of plant by taking a photo of a leaf or flower. She fizzes with the thrill of it.

'Phones know a lot! It saves the pictures too so we can look back later.'

They snap field maple, honeysuckle and cow parsley. Each time the app congratulates Cate on discovering a new species of plant, she whoops and twirls. This is childhood, too. Wonder and exploration using technology.

'I can download an app for insects and I think there's one for birdsong.'

They head down the path to sit on the front step of the holiday house.

'I saw a photograph of you and Grandfather here, in front of the door. Zach showed me. You didn't look happy.'

Imogen runs her finger over the peeling paint, then reaches up to the door-handle that hasn't changed since she was born.

'It was wonderful and awful, growing up here. I loved him very much. But I wanted my own life, too. Strange that I ended up staying. I guess it's such a huge part of me. Building the new house for me and you was a trick to allow me to remain in Halham, pretending everything had changed.'

They sit for a while in silence. Small acts could change so much. A letter to France to an absent mother to build bridges could be a start. Imogen blows slowly and smoothly from pursed lips and removes a pink envelope from her bag, handing it to Cate.

'This is for you. I've already read it, but I realise now I shouldn't have. Your friend Alana has left her address and phone number to be able to stay in contact if you'd like?'

Cate pulls the card out of the envelope and runs her fingers along the ink inside as if reading braille. Her face flushes as she nods then holds the card against her chest.

'Can we ask the phone a question? I know it can answer if you type it in.'

'You mean, like search on Google?' She doesn't know. Of course, she doesn't even know what Google is. Imogen never gave her free rein to learn about the world. What the hell has she done to her? 'What would you like to ask?'

Imogen wishes it was so simple. If she'd had an oracle at eighteen, what would she have chosen?

'Can people change their magnets?'

Another clue to Cate's strange world.

'Tell me what you mean. I'm listening.'

Cate fiddles with a fern, stroking its soft sides as she speaks. 'If there are two people but their poles are the same, then they can't ever touch. It's repulsion. It won't work even if you want it to, like my old red engine and the carriage, remember? Does the phone know if there's any way to change it?'

The air is punched out of Imogen's lungs. She'd spent most of the night revisiting places from the Rounds. The kind woman with gnarled fingers who said they hurt less after her touch. The baby with a terrible cough who fell to sleep on its mother's chest after she placed her hand over his tiny head, surprised at the softness of its scalp. The man who wouldn't say what was wrong, turned his head to the side in shame but relaxed to sleep after a few minutes of Imogen extracting the bad thing from under his skin. Was that evidence? Or was that what hope looked like; a brief respite from suffering when you believe that somebody can soothe you?

'That's not the word, Cate. Repulsion isn't the right word at all. We are tied by an invisible cord that will stretch however far we need it to and can never break, do you hear me?'

Imogen had worried so much about touch, imagining her daughter feeling obliged to spend all her time helping and healing others without a life of her own. She'd been so worried that she'd cause her daughter pain by revealing her gift. Instead, she'd caused her daughter pain by never holding her. She'd mirrored the pattern of her Father while trying to be the opposite.

'Is it okay if I try something?'

Imogen holds out her arms. Cate flings herself into the embrace. They both squeeze until it almost hurts, then laugh as Imogen covers her daughter's face and head with all the kisses she'd ever wanted to give.

They stand to face the view of Hart Hill, the final item on Cate's list of Halham's best places even though she'd never been allowed to climb it or see the world beyond.

'Would you like to go up the hill with me to see the view together?'

Cate nods. Imogen takes her daughter's hand, noticing it's almost the same size as hers now, as they make their way to the gate out of Halham.

ACKNOWLEDGEMENTS

The Bloodhound Books team took a chance on my quirky submission and helped it to become a book I'm proud of – thanks to them all, including Betsy Reavley, Tara Lyons, and editor extraordinaire Clare Law. Writing is not as solitary a pursuit as it could be when you have great support and encouragement from your friends and mentors in the writing world. My heartfelt thanks to Lilly Inkwood, Hannah Persaud, Judi Walsh, Sophie van Llewyn, Julia Kelly and Heidi James. Other friends near and far who have been so positive about my writing endeavours make the difference to keep going despite all that life throws our way. Thanks to Helen Rooney, Gemma Degg, Ruth Richards, Sam Templeman, Alison Walker, Helen Scott, Helen Rye, Victoria Richards, Joanna Saddington, Louise Mace, Curtis Hutton and Jeanette Shepherd. An early version of this book was a finalist in the TLC Pen Factor writing competition which was a boost, so my thanks to director Aki Schilz and her team.

ABOUT THE AUTHOR

Stephanie Carty is a writer and consultant clinical psychologist in the U.K. Her award-winning short fiction has been placed in international competitions and is widely published. Stephanie has published workbooks for writers on applying psychology to characters and themselves. She has a love for reading and writing across genres with a hint of the unexpected.

A NOTE FROM THE PUBLISHER

Thank you for reading this book. If you enjoyed it please do consider leaving a review on Amazon to help others find it too.

We hate typos. All of our books have been rigorously edited and proofread, but sometimes mistakes do slip through. If you have spotted a typo, please do let us know and we can get it amended within hours.

info@bloodhoundbooks.com

www.ingramcontent.com/pod-product-compliance
Lightning Source LLC
Chambersburg PA
CBHW061434210726
48287CB00007B/2215